"I think we sh

Xavier's eyes wider
faintly. "Am I imagi
marriage?"

"That's exactly what I said,

He looked incredulous.

"It would solve all our problems," she said. "Yours especially," she hurried on, "so it seems to me to be the sensible thing to do—"

"Sensible?" He raked his hair with exasperated fingers.

"You need an heir or you'll lose your half of the island to me, and unless you've got someone in mind—"

"I don't."

"Then..."

"Better the devil I know?" he suggested grimly.

"You can't buy me out—you should know that by now— and if we marry you get to keep your share."

"What's in it for you?"

"Everything," she said bluntly. And nothing, she thought. "A secure future for the islanders and the island," she insisted, ignoring the chill in his eyes. "So will you consider my suggestion?"

She had no idea what Xavier was thinking as he stared into the fire. Her best guess was that this was Xavier the businessman, weighing up the odds.

"I can't believe you're serious about this," he said, looking around at last.

"You'd have my full cooperation," she stressed, sensing the faintest of possibilities that he might say yes.

"I would certainly expect your cooperation in bed."

Wedlocked!

Conveniently wedded, passionately bedded!

Whether there's a debt to be paid, a will
to be obeyed or a business to be saved...
she's got no choice but to say "I do"!

But these billionaire grooms have got
another think coming if they imagine
the marriage will be that easy...

Soon their convenient brides become
the object of an *inconvenient* desire!

Find out what happens after the vows in

The Billionaire's Defiant Acquisition
by Sharon Kendrick

One Night to Wedding Vows by Kim Lawrence

Expecting a Royal Scandal by Caitlin Crews

Trapped by Vialli's Vows by Chantelle Shaw

Baby of His Revenge by Jennie Lucas

Look out for more ***Wedlocked!*** stories
coming soon!

Susan Stephens

A DIAMOND FOR DEL RIO'S HOUSEKEEPER

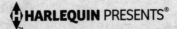

Recycling programs
for this product may
not exist in your area.

ISBN-13: 978-0-373-13485-4

A Diamond for Del Rio's Housekeeper

First North American Publication 2016

Copyright © 2016 by Susan Stephens

Printed in U.S.A.

HARLEQUIN®
www.Harlequin.com

Susan Stephens was a professional singer before meeting her husband on the Mediterranean island of Malta. In true Harlequin Presents style, they met on Monday, became engaged on Friday and married three months later. Susan enjoys entertaining, travel and going to the theater. To relax she reads, cooks and plays the piano, and when she's had enough of relaxing, she throws herself off mountains on skis or gallops through the countryside singing loudly.

Books by Susan Stephens

Harlequin Presents

In the Sheikh's Service
Bound to the Tuscan Billionaire
Master of the Desert

Hot Brazilian Nights!

In the Brazilian's Debt
At the Brazilian's Command
Brazilian's Nine Months' Notice
Back in the Brazilian's Bed

The Skavanga Diamonds

Diamond in the Desert
The Flaw in His Diamond
The Purest of Diamonds?
His Forbidden Diamond

The Acostas!

The Untamed Argentinian
The Shameless Life of Ruiz Acosta
The Argentinian's Solace
A Taste of the Untamed
The Man from Her Wayward Past
Taming the Last Acosta

Visit the Author Profile page at Harlequin.com for more titles.

For my wonderful readers, who give me license to dream. You're always at the forefront of my mind, and this is for you.

CHAPTER ONE

'THIS IS A private beach...'

Rosie had to raise her voice to reach the big, brutal-looking man lowering the anchor on his sleek black launch off shore. He'd stilled, so she was sure he'd heard her, but for some reason he'd chosen to ignore her. Waving her arms made no impact at all.

'Damned invaders,' Rosie's late elderly employer, Doña Anna, would have said as she waved her walking stick at any sailors bold enough to drop anchor near her private island. *'You can't swim here! This is my island!'* Standing belligerently, with her crab-like hands planted firmly on her bony hips, Doña Anna would continue to berate visitors—whom Rosie had always thought couldn't do much harm if all they wanted to do was enjoy the crystalline waters and sugar-sand beach for an hour or so—until they took the hint that they weren't welcome and left for kinder waters.

Rosie tensed as the man stared straight at her. With maybe fifty yards between them, his penetrating assessment stabbed her like an arrow.

Her body reacted in the craziest way, softening and yearning as the force of his personality washed over her. The effect was as powerful as if they were standing toe to toe.

She was instantly in 'fight or flight' mode. Her brain sharpened to make that call. Only what they'd called her pure, damned stubbornness at the orphanage was keeping her rooted to the spot. She might not have had the best of starts in life, but she wasn't a victim and never would be.

And a promise was a promise, Rosie vowed. Her promise to Doña Anna, that she would keep the island safe, was sacrosanct. However intimidating the man seemed, until she knew what he wanted, he wasn't getting any further than the shore.

The man had other ideas.

Her heart thundered as he sprang lightly onto the bow rail, preparing to dive into the sea. Keeping the island safe would take more than good intentions, she suspected. He was twice her size and built like a gladiator.

His dive made barely a ripple in the water. Surfacing, he powered towards the shore. There was something hard and ruthless about him that stole away her earlier confidence, replacing it with apprehension. Crew of a mother yacht generally wore some sort of uniform with the name of their boat emblazoned on it. He wore no identifying clothing. Stripped to the waist in cut-off shorts, he was maybe thirty...older than she was, anyway.

Rosie was in her early twenties. She couldn't even be sure of her date of birth. There was no record of it. A fire at the orphanage had destroyed all evidence of her history shortly after she arrived. Her life experience was limited to the strange, isolated world inside an institution, and now a small island off the southern tip of Spain.

She'd been lucky enough to be offered a job on Isla Del Rey by a charity that ran a scheme for disadvantaged young people. The post involved working on a trial basis as a companion/housekeeper for an elderly lady who had driven six previous companion/housekeepers away. On the face of it, not the most promising opportunity, but Rosie would have jumped at anything to escape the oppressive surroundings of the institution, and the island had seemed to offer sanctuary from the harsh realities of the outside world.

That world was back with a vengeance now, she thought as the man drew close to shore.

She took up position, ready to send him on his way. Doña Anna had given her so much more than a roof over her head, and she owed it to the old lady to keep her island safe.

Against all the odds, Rosie had become close to her employer, but in her wildest dreams she could never have predicted that in one last act of quite astonishing generosity Doña Anna would leave orphan Rosie Clifton half of Isla Del Rey in her will.

Rosie's inheritance became an international scandal. She hadn't been exactly welcomed into the land-owning classes, more shunned by them. Even Doña Anna's lawyer had made some excuse not to meet her. His formal letter had seemed impregnated with his scorn. How could she, a lowly housekeeper and an orphan to boot, step into the shoes of generations of Spanish aristocracy? No one had seemed to un-derstand that what Rosie had inherited was an old lady's trust, and her love.

Doña Anna's generous bequest had turned out to be a double-edged sword. Rosie had come to love the island, but without a penny to her name, and no wage coming in, she could barely afford to support herself, let alone help the islanders to market their organic produce on the mainland, as she had prom-ised them she would.

The man had reached the shallows, and was wad-ing to the shore. Naked to the waist and muscular, his deeply tanned frame dripping with seawater, he was a spectacular sight. She couldn't imagine a man like that going cap in hand for a loan.

Rosie had failed spectacularly in that direction. Every letter she'd sent to possible investors for the island had been met with silence, or scorn: *Who was she but a lowly housekeeper whose life experience was confined to an orphanage?* She couldn't even argue with that view, when it was right.

He speared her with a glance. She guessed he could open any door. But not this door. She would keep her deathbed promise to Doña Anna, and continue the fight to keep the island unspoiled. Which, in Doña Anna's language, meant no visitors—especially not a man who was looking at Rosie as if she were a piece of flotsam that had washed up on the beach. She would despatch him exactly as Doña Anna would have done, Rosie determined, standing her ground. Well, perhaps not quite the same way. She was more of a firm persuader than a shouter.

Her heart pounded with uneasiness as he strode towards her across the sand. She was alone and vulnerable. He'd chosen the best time of day to spring his surprise. Rosie had never made any secret of the fact that she liked to swim early in the morning before anyone was up. When she was alive, Doña Anna had encouraged this habit, saying Rosie should get some fresh air before spending all day in the house.

Snatching up her towel from the rock where she'd spread it out to dry, she covered herself modestly. Even so, she was hardly dressed for receiving visitors. The house was half a mile away up a steep cliff path, and no one would hear her cry for help—

She wouldn't be calling for help. She owned fifty per cent of this island, with the other fifty per cent belonging to some absentee Spanish Grandee.

Don Xavier Del Rio was Doña Anna's nephew, but as he hadn't troubled to visit his aunt during Rosie's time on the island, not even attending her funeral, Rosie doubted he would inconvenience himself now. According to Doña Anna, he was a playboy who lived life on the edge. As far as Rosie was concerned, he was a hard-hearted brute, who didn't deserve such a lovely aunt.

Admittedly, when it came to his business, he seemed to be successful. But, billionaire or not, in Rosie's view, he should have made some effort to visit Doña Anna—or perhaps he was just too important to care.

He couldn't believe what he was seeing. The girl had set herself up on the beach as if he were the intruder. 'You're right,' he barked at her. 'This *is* a private beach. So what the hell are you doing here?'

'I own—I mean, I live on the island,' she said, tipping her chin a little higher in what he supposed was an attempt to stare him in the eyes.

He towered over her. She was small and young and lithe, with long, striking red hair, and an expression that appeared candid, but was most definitely defiant and determined. She was pale, but outwardly composed. He knew who she was. The lawyer had warned him she might be difficult and not to be deceived by her innocent looks.

'Did the lawyer send you?' she challenged, seeming to have no guard on her tongue.

'No one *sent* me,' he replied, all the time assessing her keenly.

'Then why are you here?'

Her clenched fists were the only sign that she was nervous. She had courage to stand up to him, but he wasn't a bully and she was a young girl alone on the beach. He ordered his muscles to stand down. 'I'm here to see you.'

'Me?'

She put one small hand on the swell of plump breasts peeping above the towel. And then a stiff breeze caught hold of her hair and lifted it, tossing it about. The urge to fist a hank of it, so he could ease her head back and kiss her throat, was overwhelming.

She might hold appeal, but anyone who could persuade his crotchety aunt to leave them such a sizeable bequest had to be more conniving than she looked.

'We have business to discuss.' He glanced up the cliff towards the house.

'You can only be one person,' she said, levelling her cool amethyst gaze on him. 'The lawyers have shown no interest in me, or in the island. They're happy to let Isla Del Rey go to hell, and me with it. Every door in the city's been slammed in my face. But I suppose you already know that…Don Xavier.'

He remained impassive. The day the contents of his aunt's will had become known her lawyers had been in touch with him to profess their undying loyalty. The firm had worked for the Del Rio family for years, the head of the firm was at pains to remind him, and every associate was squarely behind Don Xavier in this most *regrettable* situation. There was a good case to challenge the will, the lawyer had assured him, no doubt rubbing his hands with glee at the thought of more fees to come. Xavier had dismissed the man's suggestion out of hand. He would deal with the situation, as he would deal with this girl.

'Are you responsible for me being ignored in the city?' the girl now challenged him, firming her jaw with affront.

'No,' he said honestly. His aunt had always been mischievous, and never more so than when she had drawn up her will. Now he'd met the girl with whom he shared the bequest, he suspected Doña Anna must have taken much pleasure in putting as many obstacles in his way as she could before he could lay claim to an island that was rightfully his. 'No doubt the money men think as I do, that the responsibility of Isla Del Rey cannot rest in the hands of one young girl.'

'Well, I don't suppose you're interested in my opinion,' she flashed back.

She was going to give it to him anyway, he suspected.

She proved him right. 'Anyone lucky enough to have relatives should cherish them, not abandon them, however difficult they might be.'

'Was that a dig at me?' he asked with mild amusement. 'Are you suggesting that I have as little claim to the island as you?'

'You have the name,' she conceded. 'You also have the reputation. Why would your aunt leave the island she loved above all things to a man as notorious as you?'

The bluntness of this statement silenced him for a moment, and he had to admit to some grudging respect. Her boldness was shocking, but it was also refreshing. He guessed her blunt character had been forged on the anvil of a difficult childhood. She'd had to find ways to survive, and had chosen logic and stubbornness over compliance and self-pity. She was brave. He'd give her that. Not many people would take him on.

'No argument, Don Xavier?'

He raised a brow, but what she'd said was true. His reputation hung by a thread. He lived hard and fast, funded by the lifestyle his highly successful business ventures provided. He wasn't interested in love and caring. They had only brought him disappointment in the past. He had no time for such things now. That was why he had avoided both the island and his aunt. He wasn't proud to admit that the thought of rekindling the feelings he'd had for the old lady when he was a boy had made it easier for him to stay away. His parents had knocked all thoughts of love out of him. More grief? More regret? Why would he invite them in? He'd done what Doña Anna had asked him to do, which was to make more money to fund those schemes she would have been proud of, and that had to be enough.

But his mischievous aunt was asking more of him in her will. He could only imagine she had been playing games with him when she had added a particular caveat that stood in the way of him claiming his inheritance.

'I imagine it's the terms of your aunt's will that brought you here,' the girl commented forthrightly.

What business was it of hers?

Against his better judgement, his senses stirred as she continued to interrogate him with her astonishingly beautiful amethyst eyes.

'We're both here for the same reason, I imagine,' he countered evenly. 'To sort out the terms of the bequest.'

'I live here, you don't,' she said, smiling a faint challenge at him.

Was she staking her claim? If she'd read the will, and he presumed she had, she would know he could forfeit his half of the island if he didn't provide the estate with an heir within two years. It must have amused his aunt to put his infamous reputation to the test.

'You're under some pressure, I imagine,' the girl said.

Seeing the glint of amusement in her eyes, he guessed she was enjoying this as much as his aunt must have done. He could imagine them getting on together. And of course the girl could afford to laugh, as her fifty per cent of the island was safe. All she had to do was wait him out, hope he didn't produce an heir, and she would own the island outright. His trump card was the fact that she didn't have any money to support herself, so nothing was certain. Not yet.

'So you're familiar with the terms of my aunt's will?' he confirmed as they stood facing each other, weighing each other up.

'Yes,' she said frankly. 'Your aunt's lawyer was difficult to begin with. He didn't want to show me anything, but I insisted.'

I bet you did, he thought.

'He couldn't deny my request,' she explained. 'To be honest, I just wanted to see your aunt's will with my own eyes to confirm that I really had inherited half of Isla Del Rey, but then...' Biting down on her lip, she looked away.

'Yes?' he prompted, sensing serious thoughts beneath her calm exterior. The worst mistake he could make would be to take this woman lightly.

'But then I read that bit about you,' she said, refocusing her luminous stare on his face. 'So I understand the pressure you're under.' She couldn't resist a little smile as she added, 'I always knew Doña Anna had a strange sense of humour, but I have to admit she excelled herself this time. Maybe if you hadn't ignored her for so long—'

'I stand reprimanded,' he said curtly. He didn't want to discuss his aunt with anyone, let alone this young woman.

'The thing I find confusing,' she said, 'is this. I always thought Doña Anna believed in family. At least, that was the impression she gave me, but now it seems she was hell-bent on punishment.' She screwed her eyes up as she thought about it.

And they were still beautiful.

'Punishing me, not you,' he said.

'But still…' She stared at him with interest for a good few moments. 'You must have really rattled her cage. But you did, by staying away so long.'

She wasn't frightened of speaking her mind. The more he saw of her, the more she intrigued him. His original intention had been to send her sailing away from the island on a raft made of money. He doubted now he'd met her that she'd stand for that. She was intelligent and defiant, and also extremely attractive.

That sort of interest could get in his way. He couldn't allow distractions like this girl to knock him off course. She was right about the will throwing everything into chaos. Doña Anna, of all people, should have known his limitations. He could make money hand over fist, but he'd make a lousy parent. Why try to saddle some poor child with a father who was incapable of feeling?

'We'd better go to the house,' he said, turning to the main point of his visit.

'What? No,' she said.

'I beg your pardon?' He swung around to see her digging her little toes into the sand.

'You should have contacted me in the usual way—to arrange a meeting that didn't involve a confrontation on the beach at dawn,' she explained, frowning at him.

He dipped his head to hide a smile. People had been known to try and bribe his PA to secure a few minutes of his time. Rosie Clifton, on the other hand, was only short of his aunt's walking stick to wave in his face as she did her best to drive him away. But her time was up now. However appealing he might find her, he was a busy man.

'I said, no!'

He gazed at her with incredulity as she took the few steps necessary to dodge in front of him and block his way. 'It's not convenient,' she explained, holding her ground.

Not convenient for him to tour *his* house, his island? An astonishing number of doors might have opened in the recent past for orphaned Rosie Clifton, but no door had ever closed in his face. He would visit his house, and he would tour his island. And then he would decide what to do about the girl.

'Perhaps another time?' she tempered, reacting to his thunderous expression no doubt. 'Some time soon?' she offered with the hint of a smile.

Her charm was wasted on him. 'Some time now,' he insisted, moving past her.

CHAPTER TWO

HE SHOULD HAVE known she'd race after him. When she grabbed hold of his arm, he felt the power of those tiny fingers as clearly as if they were stroking his groin. The thought of those hands clutching him in the throes of passion was enough to stop him dead in his tracks. Her touch was electrifying. And then there was her spirit. Rosie Clifton might not possess a fraction of his wealth or power, but she knew no fear. It was impossible for him not to admire her just a little.

'You can come up to the house another time,' she said, still hanging on to his arm as she stared up into his face. 'We'll make a proper appointment. I promise.'

'Will we?' he demanded with irony.

As he stared down her amethyst eyes darkened, confirming his growing suspicion that the attraction between them was mutual. And inconvenient, he reminded himself firmly. He wasn't here for seduction. He had business with Rosie Clifton.

'Neither of us is dressed for a formal meeting,' she pointed out. 'We won't feel comfortable. And when there are such important things to discuss…'

He awarded her a point for a good, persuasive argument.

'So…?' Her beautifully drawn lips parted as she waited for his answer.

'So I'll come back,' he agreed.

'Thank you,' she exclaimed with relief.

It was an error on his part. He had given her chance to prepare for *the next time*. His aunt must be laughing in her grave. Doña Anna couldn't have planned this better, placing two people with the same aim—one an idealist, and the other a business mogul—in direct conflict with each other. Inwardly, he huffed a smile of admiration. He had to admit, this sort of mischief was right up her street.

'Before you go…' She nibbled on her lip.

'Yes?'

'I want you to know that I really loved your aunt.'

He shrugged. Should he care? Was she waiting for him to make some comment to echo this? He examined his feelings scrupulously and came up with nothing. The numbness inside him had been there since childhood, he supposed. He didn't know how he felt about his aunt, though he might have known that nothing short of a dynasty would satisfy Doña Anna.

'Your aunt brought you up, didn't she?' Rosie pressed.

'Only because my parents preferred the fleshpots of Monte Carlo,' he said with an impatient gesture that told her to leave the subject alone.

'That must have hurt you,' she said gently, as if she cared.

'It was a long time ago.' He frowned, hoping that would put her off.

It seemed to. She didn't say anything more on the subject, but she looked at him with something close to pity, which annoyed him even more.

'Your aunt said she threw you out when you were a teenager.' She laughed, seeming to find this amusing. 'She said it was the best thing she ever did for you—but then she was always teaching people lessons, including me.'

'But not the type of lesson that would include holding your tongue,' he murmured dryly.

She ignored him and continued. 'Doña Anna said old money doesn't last for ever, and that it's up to each new generation to make its own luck in life. Which you've done in shedloads.' Her eyes widened with admiration.

Only her innocence and complete lack of sophistication could allow for this, he thought as she went on to list his credentials. 'First you made a fortune in the tech world, and then you made a second fortune building six-star hotels across the world with state-of-the-art golf courses attached.' She frowned. 'I imagine that's why your aunt left me half the island—to stop you rampaging over here. Rumour says you're a billionaire,' she added with startling candour.

'I don't much care about that.'

'She told me that too,' she called after him as he began to stroll away from her towards the sea.

'Was there anything she didn't tell you?' he said, stopping in his tracks.

'Oh, I'm sure there were lots of things she left out...'

He could only hope.

'Did she speak about me often?' he asked. He was suddenly filled with a need to know. He felt a pang of regret as he asked the question, which was a first for him.

'She did talk about you—quite a lot,' Rosie revealed brightly, and with no malice he could detect. 'I'm sorry if I've upset you,' she said as he turned away.

'You haven't upset me.' Pausing beside one of the gargantuan rocks on the beach, he leaned back against its smooth surface. Like it or not, the girl had brought the past back into clear focus.

'I should get back,' she said.

'Do you swim here every day?' he said, turning to look at her. Suddenly, he wasn't so keen for her to go.

'Every morning—I have done ever since I arrived on the island. Such a luxury,' she said. Rolling her head back, she closed her eyes as if she was reliving each and every moment she'd spent in the surf.

The island must have been a revelation to her after the orphanage. He couldn't imagine being brought up in an institution with no personal interest lavished on a person at all. At least he'd had Doña Anna. He was almost glad now that fate had intervened for Rosie Clifton. He would have had to be a heartless monster not to.

A visit to the orphanage by the royal patron of one of the charities he sponsored had led to Rosie being singled out. The prince had told Xavier that this particular girl had caught his attention because of her calm and resilient manner. He wondered now if Rosie's luminous appearance had attracted the prince's attention. That, and her obvious innocence. When the prince had first mentioned Rosie, he had thought immediately of his aunt and the possibility that a young girl might succeed where so many older, professional carers had failed. Never in his wildest dreams had he imagined that Rosie Clifton would be quite so successful. He searched now for guile beneath the frankness of her stare, and found none. 'Do you swim on your own in the sea?'

'Why not?' she countered pertly. 'You did.'

When she cocked her head to issue the challenge, she somehow managed to look more appealing than ever. It was time to rein in his feelings before they started to cloud his judgement. 'Do you think that's wise?' he said, turning stern. 'What if you got into trouble in the water?'

'I can get into trouble on the land just as easily,' she said.

As she masked her smile it was hard not to like her, which was everything he had vowed not to do. When she shrugged, drawing his attention to the womanly frame beneath the tightly bound towel, and to her slender shoulders with their sprinkling of freckles like gold dust on her skin, he knew he was in trouble.

'One thing I learned as a child,' she added frankly, 'was how to keep my head above water.'

'I have no doubt of that,' he agreed as she tossed her hair back, sending the glistening waves cascading in a fiery cloud almost to her waist. 'But you're taking a big risk with your safety,' he warned.

'It's not such a big deal if you know the seas around the island, is it, Don Xavier…?'

'Touché,' he murmured to himself. 'You're right,' he admitted. 'I swam here many times as a boy, but that doesn't make it safe for you.'

'Are you saying you're a better swimmer than I am?' There was both challenge and humour in her eyes now.

'Enough!' he insisted, knowing it was time to end this before she won him over completely. 'Allow me to introduce myself formally. Don Xavier Del Rio, at your service…'

'I doubt that somehow.' She laughed. 'And I don't want you to be at my service. But I am pleased to *formally* meet you at last,' she teased him. 'Perhaps we can start over?' She suggested this hopefully, extending a hand for him to shake. 'Rosie Clifton,' she declared, 'at no one's service.'

He laughed. 'There's never been the slightest doubt of that.'

As he brushed his lips against the back of her hand he felt her tremble. When he let her go, she quickly put her hands behind her back, as if to keep them out of mischief. She wasn't so good at hiding her feelings, after all. He didn't intimidate her. She didn't feel particularly antagonistic towards him. She was naturally wary and inquisitive, but when he touched her, she was aroused. He wondered what new discoveries he would make about Rosie Clifton. Compliance must have been her best defence at the orphanage, and she would have had to be accommodating to keep her job with his aunt. She must have worked out by now that half an island was of no use to either of them, and he was curious as to where she thought they'd go from here. 'What do you know about me, Rosie?'

'Probably as much as you know about me,' she said frankly. 'I know you by reputation, of course. Who doesn't? But as that's only hearsay and I like to draw my own conclusions about people, I'm keeping an open mind right now.'

'Should I thank you for that?'

'Do as you like,' she said easily. 'I do know that everything you've achieved in life, you've done without anyone's help. Doña Anna told me that too,' she explained, unintentionally twisting the knife in the wound she'd inadvertently opened. He'd had enough of this. She was getting under his skin, making him feel too much. He couldn't have that. 'But that doesn't tell me who you are, or if I can trust you—'

He sidestepped her and made for the house.

'Hey!' She chased after him as he headed for the cliff path. And, *Dios*, now she was standing in front of him.

'Get out of my way, please,' he instructed quietly.

'No.' Folding her arms, she said loud and clear, 'You're not going a step further. I told you already, it's not convenient for you to visit the house.'

He could swing her over his shoulder and carry her there, but that would lead to nowhere good for Rosie Clifton, and maybe life had beat up on her enough. She was far too young and too innocent for him, with his sophisticated tastes in the bedroom. She featured nowhere on his agenda, other than to buy her off.

'I said no,' she warned again, when he went to move past her.

He stopped. She amused him. Her lips might be kissable, but they were currently set in such a firm, determined line. And now another question occurred to him: Was Rosie Clifton really as innocent as she looked? Had she been swept along by circumstances beyond her control, or was she a consummate actress who had managed to fool his aunt? Tricksters didn't tend to have *swindler* tattooed on their brow. Either way, he would deal with Ms Clifton. If nothing more than good fortune and happy fate shone on Rosie Clifton, then a financial settlement to make her eyes water would soon get rid of her. If she was an idealist who believed she was saving the island from a ruthless playboy entrepreneur, namely him, then his cantankerous aunt had indeed met her match, and there would be trouble ahead—but not for him.

'If you don't get out of my way, I shall have to move you.'

Just the thought of taking that lithe, rebellious body in his arms was enough to whip his senses into an agony of lust, but she just laughed. 'I'd like to see you try,' she said.

He held up his hands, palms flat. He could wait. Except for the issue of the heir—he held all the cards and she held none. She couldn't fight him through the courts. She lacked the money to do so. She was at his mercy. Even if he failed to produce an heir and his half reverted to her, she'd never have the money to continue to manage the island. Whichever way she turned, there was no future for Rosie Clifton on the island. The only fight she could put up was with words. They both knew the outcome was inevitable. He would own one hundred per cent of Isla Del Rey. It was just a matter of time. But there was no mileage in making her miserable.

'Try to be reasonable,' he suggested. 'It's important that I see the house as soon as possible to make an initial assessment of the changes that need to be made.'

'What changes?' she retorted. 'The hacienda is perfectly serviceable as it stands.'

Rosie doubted anything had been refurbished or rearranged since the man who was making her body yearn for things it could hardly imagine had lived there as a boy. She had always thought the old house perfect. It wore the patina of age and regular use with such comfortable ease, reflecting everything that was cosy and special about the home Doña Anna had made for them both. What right did he have to come storming in, talking about change?

'The sooner the better,' he repeated, in what she gathered was his best attempt at a pleasant tone. He failed to charm her.

'I'm afraid that won't be possible,' she stated firmly.

He moved past her, but she caught up with him again. If it was possible for a man to grow taller and become more intimidating, he'd just done that.

'You can't keep me away for ever.' His stern eyes heated every part of her, and, instead of resenting him, she found to her bemusement that she was excited. 'Or had you forgotten I also own fifty per cent of this island?' he demanded.

'I haven't forgotten anything,' she said, especially the bizarre terms of Doña Anna's will. No wonder he was so angry. Those terms had left her flailing for the necessary finance to remain living on the island, and him needing an heir. She might be at her wits' end, but his buccaneering lifestyle had been cut off at the root. 'All I'm suggesting is a rain check. When we've both calmed down and we're properly dressed for the occasion, I'd be pleased to show you around.'

Reason had always worked best for Rosie when she had encountered difficult situations at the orphanage. If there was one thing that living in an institution had taught her, it was the basic rules of survival. The most important rule of all was to make no ripples, and if she did, to smooth them over fast.

She shivered involuntarily as Don Xavier's black stare licked over her. Her almost naked body was eager for more of his attention. Thankfully, she had more sense.

'My PA will be in touch,' he said coolly. 'Once I've had a chance to inspect both the island and the hacienda, you will be invited to the mainland for a meeting, where we will discuss terms.'

What terms? When did she agree to this?

His dismissive gesture now suggested that it would be more convenient still if he could brush her under the table along with everything else he found superfluous in his life. She had no intention of going to the mainland for a meeting. His terms? His territory? She might be young, but she wasn't stupid.

'I'm not sure that will be convenient for me,' she said bluntly. 'And, as far as I'm aware, we have nothing to discuss. The terms of the will are quite clear.'

His expression blackened to a frightening degree. This was a man who wasn't used to anyone disagreeing with him, she gathered.

'Are you marooned on the island?' he thundered.

'No, but I have a lot on.'

'Such as?' he derided. 'You've no funds—no income.'

'I can accomplish a lot with hard work and no money,' she argued. 'And just because I've been turned down by lenders to date, doesn't mean I'm giving up. I don't think your aunt would give up. And I don't think Doña Anna would leave me half this island unless she was confident I could sort things out.'

'Your intention is to help the islanders market their organic produce, I believe?'

He was well informed. 'Why not?' She might as well put her stake in the ground now.

Maybe it would be better to soften her attitude and try to engage his support? Her main goal was to help the islanders, not herself, and if she didn't control her feelings—feelings she usually had no trouble controlling—the next deputation to the island might include Don Xavier's legal team.

Correct. And she couldn't risk that. She had no funds to fight him. It was time to swallow her pride and make him feel welcome. Maybe if they worked at it they could find a solution together. She was no good at dressing things up, so she just said the first thing that came into her head. 'If you come back tomorrow I'll make you some ice cream.'

The look he gave her suggested she might as well have invited him to join her in a bondage session, complete with whips and masks.

'Three o'clock tomorrow,' he rapped. 'And no ice cream.'

CHAPTER THREE

THE FOLLOWING DAY, Rosie's heart was pounding with anticipation as she waited for Don Xavier to arrive. He might be cold and arrogant, but she was thrilled at the thought of seeing him again. She didn't have much excitement in her life, but she'd always been a dreamer. And today Don Xavier was playing the starring role. Maybe it was his need for an heir that had stirred her imagination. How was he going to get one? The usual way, obviously—but with whom? He probably had hordes of glamorous girlfriends, but she couldn't imagine him settling down.

In honour of his visit she was wearing her one good dress. She'd bought it in a thrift shop with the small allowance she'd received from the prince's charity. The money was supposed to help her to prepare for her first placement. She'd spent most of it on books to help her understand the needs of the elderly, and the rest on ice cream as she worried about whether or not she'd be up to the job.

The dress was yellow, with a floating cotton skirt

and fitted top. The colour didn't do much for her freckled complexion and it clashed with her flaming red hair, but there hadn't been much choice in her size. It was old-fashioned, but had seemed to Rosie's untrained eye to be the type of dress that wouldn't alarm an elderly lady searching for a discreet companion. Predictably, Doña Anna had hated it, calling it Rosie's custard dress, but Rosie still thought it was pretty and low-key.

She stared out of the kitchen window, wondering if Don Xavier had changed his mind. Maybe his people would arrive instead, and try to drive her away. Her pulse raced with anger at the thought. He'd better come back and face her.

So far the sea was placid blue, and decidedly empty. There was no sleek black launch approaching, and no impossibly good-looking Spanish visitor powering through the waves towards her. But she was ready for whatever came next. She had cleaned the house from top to bottom, and was satisfied that it had never looked better. He couldn't fail to be impressed. She had always longed for a house of her own to care for, and saw the work as a privilege rather than drudgery. And she would gladly kick her pride into touch if she could persuade him to give her a loan to help the islanders launch their plan to market their produce worldwide.

The more she reflected on this, the more she wondered about Doña Anna's intentions when she drew up her will. Was this one last attempt to save Don

Xavier from his empty, meaningless life? Or was that Rosie being romantic again? In her view, all the money in the world couldn't buy the love and support of a family, and, if Don Xavier had only known it, Doña Anna had been waiting to welcome him back into her family home with open arms.

Brushing her hair away from her face, Rosie pulled away from the window. It looked as if he wasn't coming. Her gaze lingered on the flowers she'd cut fresh from the garden that morning… Iceberg roses: pure white and lightly scented. The full, fat blooms thrived in clusters, just like the best families, she mused, smiling at the analogy. Not that she was an expert on either families or roses. The reason she loved the roses was for the way they thrust their scented heads so proudly above the weeds she hadn't got round to pulling out yet. There were so many things on the island worth preserving.

Isla Del Rey had bewitched Rosie from the moment she'd stepped onshore. She had been instantly dazzled by the island's beauty. It was so warm and sunny after the dreary cold of the city-centre orphanage where she'd grown up. There were sugar-sand beaches and vibrant colours everywhere, instead of unrelieved grey. And so much space and clean air to breathe. She had left a grimy city behind, and with it the restrictions of the orphanage. On the island, for the very first time in her life, she'd felt free. Best of all, she loved the people for the way they smiled and waved at her, as if they wanted to welcome her to their beautiful island home. Their cause had been her cause ever since.

Perhaps the biggest treat of all when she'd arrived had been the discovery that she would have a room to herself. And it was such a beautiful room. Light and spacious, Rosie's new bedroom overlooked the ocean, which was like a dream come true. Another favourite place in the hacienda was the library, where Doña Anna had encouraged Rosie to read any book she liked. That was when Rosie had suggested reading to the old lady. From that day on they had shared many adventures together, and, even if those adventures were confined to the pages of a book, Rosie credited storytelling with bringing them closer.

The varying tales had prompted Doña Anna to reveal so many episodes from her life. Rosie's experience of love and life had been practically zero up to then, but reading to Doña Anna had awoken in her a love for family, and a longing for the type of romance she was reading about in books. Love grew between the two of them during these regular sessions in the library. It made Rosie long for children of her own, so she could tell them about Doña Anna, and keep the memory of a very special woman alive. Her dream was that her children would pass on that memory to their children, so they would understand how lives could be turned around if just one person cared enough to make a difference.

When Doña Anna asked Rosie to stay on, making what was originally supposed to be a temporary position as housekeeper/companion permanent, it was the happiest day of her life. And the easiest decision she'd ever had to make, Rosie remembered. Doña Anna was the mother figure she'd never known. She loved the old lady for her prickly kindness, and for her generous heart.

She would always love her, Rosie reflected as she glanced at her wristwatch and frowned for the umpteenth time.

He glanced at the clock and ground his jaw. He had never been so impatient to get away from a meeting before, but he was itching to get back to the island.

And whose fault was that?

A pale, determined face, framed by a fiery cloud of shimmering red hair, came to mind. He resolutely blanked it. The last thing he needed was for the basest form of primal instinct to colour his renowned detachment.

And then there was Isla Del Rey, and his conflicting memories of the island, to further muddy the water. While ideas were batted between his team, he thought back. As a youth he had loathed the island for its restrictions. As a boy, he had associated the place with loneliness and disappointment, which was only made bearable thanks to the intervention of his aunt.

In fairness to his parents, they had never professed to love him. They never tired of telling him that he was both an accident and an inconvenience. Hope that they would one day learn to love him had taken

a long time to die. He'd come home from school full
of excitement at the thought of seeing them again,
only to find them ready to leave as he arrived. Or
they would promise to come and not turn up at all.

One day his mother told him to his face that
everything he touched turned to dust. She'd been
a beauty before he was born, loved by his father
and feted by the world, but now, thanks to her son,
Xavier, she was nothing. He had destroyed her. And
when his seven-year-old self had begged her not to
say such things, clinging to her hand as she left the
room, she had shaken him off with disgust, and then
laughed in his face when he'd started crying. No
wonder he'd steered clear of romantic entanglements.
He'd seen where they led.

Doña Anna had stepped into the breach, raising
him, and encouraging him to make the best of the
island—to swim around it, and to sail around it—
and he'd enjoyed his first love affair on the beach.
But though his aunt had told him on numerous occasions that his mother's words were just the emotional
outpourings of a troubled woman, those ugly words
still rang in his head. He wasn't capable of love. He
was a jinx, a misfortune. He destroyed love—

He turned as Margaret, his second in command,
coughed discreetly to attract his attention. 'You want
these plans acted upon right away, Xavier?'

'That's right,' he confirmed.

She knew he'd been remembering. Margaret had

an uncanny knack of sensing when he was wrestling the demons from the past.

'And you want that done *before* you attempt a satisfactory settlement with Rosie Clifton?'

'Do you doubt I'll reach a settlement with the girl?'

Everyone but Margaret laughed at his remark. Margaret had read the will, so she knew he had to produce an heir. Two years was no time at all, she'd told him with concern written all over her face. What was he supposed to do? Pluck one out of thin air? The thought of breeding with one of the women he customarily dated held no appeal at all.

'I think this is a tricky situation of a type we haven't encountered before,' Margaret now commented thoughtfully.

Tricky was the understatement of the year.

'If you mean Ms Clifton fires on emotion, while I work solely with the facts, then you're probably right,' he conceded. 'But surely, that guarantees a satisfactory outcome for our side?'

Whether Margaret agreed or not, he would go ahead with his plans. Who was going to stand in his way? Not Rosie Clifton, that was for sure—

Rosie Clifton...

He couldn't get her out of his head. Just her name was enough to set his senses raging. He suspected that beneath her composure Señorita Clifton could whip up quite a storm...

'I've never known you to be so distracted at a meeting,' Margaret commented discreetly.

He noticed everyone was leaving the room, while he had been thinking about Rosie Clifton. He was glad there was an air of excitement. His team was like a pack of greyhounds in the traps, eager to chase up every detail in his plan.

'You're right,' he agreed, standing to hold Margaret's chair. 'I've got a lot on my mind.'

Women had always been ornaments in the past, to be enjoyed and briefly admired. He had never thought of them as potential mothers to any children he might have. He'd never thought of having children, or settling down. Life had kicked that notion out of him. His best plan was to make Rosie Clifton an offer for her half of the island that she couldn't possibly refuse.

She might refuse.

There was that possibility, he conceded now he'd met her. The figure he had in mind was substantial, but would she take it? She was an idealist with her own plans for the island. She knew his reputation for taking wasteland and transforming it into a site of unparalleled luxury, but to Rosie every inch of that island held magic and potential—and not for a six-star hotel.

'Xavier...'

'Yes, Margaret?' He would trust this woman with his life. She was the only woman he would trust with his fortune. Margaret was his fifty-four-year-old financial director, an accountant with a steel-trap mind who could run circles around every bean counter he knew. It was thanks to Margaret that he could take time away from the business. As a judge of people she had no equal. What would Margaret make of Señorita Clifton? he wondered.

'I knew the meeting might run over,' she said as he held the door for her, 'and so I took the liberty of ordering the chopper to be fuelled and ready for you. You can leave at once.'

Margaret's second talent was for reading his mind. His mood lifted, and he smiled at her decadent English vowels. Years of drilling in a strict UK boarding school accounted for the precision of her accent, Margaret had once told him. He didn't care. He'd forgive her anything. She was the one woman in his life who had never disappointed him. Nodding briefly, he smiled his thanks and then they both went their separate ways.

It was late afternoon. Rosie was sitting on the beach, staring out to sea as she dabbled her feet in the water. She kept telling herself she knew Don Xavier wouldn't come.

She should be relieved he wasn't coming. She wasn't relieved. Part of her wanted to get their business over with as fast as she could, while another, far less worthy part of her just wanted to see him again. Her best guess was that he couldn't admit—not even to himself—that the island still meant something to him, and so he had decided to stay away. She got that. She had difficulty with emotions, having hidden hers for years. She would have been laughed at when she lived at the orphanage if she had given away even a hint of her romantic dreams, but that had never stopped her dreaming. In fact, sometimes, she thought she was overburdened with dreams, but they had never turned her into a block of ice like Don Xavier.

Almost six o'clock! The day was flying away. It was time to go back to the house. The glaring light of a sultry Spanish afternoon was fast burning out to burnished gold. The sunset promised to be spectacular, which was the only thing holding her on the beach. The sky was an intense, almost metallic blue, while the first signs of dusk were appearing on the horizon in random drifts of fluffy pink clouds. The sea was so smooth it looked like a skating rink, as if the waves, having exerted themselves all day, couldn't be bothered to crash on the shore, so they were creeping up it instead. She scrunched her toes in the wet sand, loving the sensation as she allowed the rhythmical sound of the waves to flitter across her eardrums. Even that wasn't soothing. Her irritation about the missing guest was stronger. Don Xavier seemed to find it easy to walk away from things and she'd been looking forward to another verbal sparring match with him. They had to get together if they were going to sort out the future of the island, and they should do that as soon as possible. They had a duty to the islanders.

She had wanted a chance to make him understand how much she cared for the island, and how lucky she felt to have been given the chance to live here. Helping the islanders was just her way of thanking them for their kindness towards her. Her dream was to share the island one day with other young people who'd had no advantages in life. She guessed that would have to wait, as her tiny pot of money would run out soon—

A sound distracted her. She couldn't identify it at first. Then she realised it was the sound of rotor blades approaching fast. As she sprang to her feet a gleaming black craft appeared over the cliff at the far end of the bay. She remained motionless as it wheeled onto its side, at what appeared to her to be an impossibly acute angle.

She exhaled with relief when it levelled off to skim the surface of the sea, driving up spumes of water in glittering clouds. It kept on coming towards her, and only wheeled away at the very last minute. Rising rapidly, it banked steeply before turning inland. The pilot seemed to be flying on the edge of what was possible.

So it could only be one man, Rosie reasoned. Who else would take such risks with his life and company property?

And she shouldn't be here on the beach daydream-

ing, but up at the house ready to greet him—or to
hold him off!

To hell with greeting him! She should be up at
the house to establish her right to call the hacienda
home—the only home she'd ever known. More importantly, the hacienda had meant everything to
Doña Anna, and no patronising, nose-in-the-air
grandee was going to bulldoze it, to build yet another of his glitzy hotels. Kicking off her flip-flops,
she began to run.

Rosie scrambled up the cliff path as if the hounds
of hell were after her, and she didn't stop until she
reached the boundary to the property—a fence she
hadn't realised was quite so broken down. She picked
her way carefully through the broken struts of a bar-
rier that was supposed to divide a once beautiful formal garden from the glorious wilderness. As of now,
it was all glorious wilderness, she saw with concern.

Imagining Don Xavier seeing the same thing
made Rosie wince. She'd known things were bad,
but not this bad. She'd meant to do something about
the garden, but had no money to pay a gardener, and
there was so much to do inside the house. Any spare
time she had was spent researching grants and sub-
sidies for the islanders, to help them get their plans
for marketing their organic produce off the ground.

She glanced up to see the helicopter hovering over
the hacienda. It looked like a giant black hand come
to claim its rightful property. Its shadow was like an
omen. Descending slowly from the sky, it looked like

a malevolent locust as it settled on its widespread skids. It seemed to Rosie to be the clearest signal yet that she had no money, no power, no influence, while Don Xavier Del Rio had a cash register for a heart. What was going to happen to the island if she didn't stand firm? Why had Doña Anna set them against each other like this? She couldn't have expected them to work together. Don Xavier would never consider it. Doña Anna hadn't been exactly noted for her willingness to compromise, and yet that was what she expected them to do.

So was she going to disappoint the woman who had given her a fresh chance in life?

Drawing a deep steadying breath, Rosie smoothed her hair and straightened her dress, ready for her second meeting with Don Xavier.

CHAPTER FOUR

THE KITCHEN DOOR was open so he walked straight in. It smelled clean, but looked shabby. He leaned over the pristine sink to see if the window really was in as much danger of falling out as he'd first thought. He heard a faint noise behind him—just a breath, a slight shift in the air. He turned and she was there.

His good intentions counted for nothing. His body responded instantly to the sight of Rosie Clifton, his groin tightening as blood ripped through his veins. She was so young, so innocent—and so not his type, but it seemed that no argument he could put up could take anything away from her appeal. The low-slanting sun was shining straight into her face. She looked like an angel waiting to fall, in shades of white and gold—and yellow? As she came deeper into the kitchen he took more notice of the dress. It was a hideous dress that must have hung unloved in a thrift shop for years, but on Señorita Clifton it served a very definite purpose, which was to cling to her shapely form with loving attention to detail.

'Don Xavier,' she exclaimed in a calm, clear voice, walking forward to greet him.

'Señorita Clifton.' His tone was cool.

'Rosie, please,' she insisted, forming the words with the kissable lips he hadn't been able to get out of his mind.

'Rosie.' He inclined his head slightly in acknowledgement of her arrival, and then he remained still, waiting for her to come to him.

He could try every trick in the book, but she was never dismayed. The power of her easy-going personality was undeniable. As she extended her tiny hand for him to shake, she tipped up her chin to look him in the eyes, and he felt the force of that stare in his groin, which didn't just tighten now, but ached with the most urgent need.

'Welcome to Hacienda de Rio,' she said with a smile, as if he were the interloper. And then, having realised her mistake, instead of blushing or showing how awkward she surely must feel at the blunder, she put her hand over her mouth and giggled before exclaiming, 'That was a bit of a clanger, wasn't it?'

He stared coolly into her eyes, trying to read her. He could read every woman he'd ever met, from the mother who had barely made eye contact with him, to Doña Anna's scathing and ironic stare, and, after them, the legions of women who knew very well how to flirt with their eyes; they were all transparent to him, but Rosie Clifton was an enigma, and she intrigued him. She was also extremely self-possessed for a girl from nowhere, who had owned nothing but the clothes she stood up in until a few weeks ago.

Seeing the cold suspicion in his eyes, she had taken a step back. Feeling the table behind her legs, she reached behind her to rest her palms on the scrubbed pine surface, making her breasts appear more prominent than ever. Had any other woman done the same thing, he might have wondered if it was an invitation, but Rosie Clifton only succeeded in making herself look younger and more vulnerable than ever. Perhaps that too was a ploy of sorts, he reflected.

'So, you got here at last?' she challenged him lightly.

He shrugged. 'I came as soon as I could.'

She pressed her lips together in a wry, accepting smile. 'Your aunt mentioned that you're a workaholic.'

He had forgotten how self-possessed she was. But now there was a faint blush on her face, and her amethyst eyes had darkened. He watched her breathing quicken, displaying the shape of her full breasts quite graphically in the close-fitting dress.

'This is, of course, as much your home as mine,' she said candidly.

'How kind of you to say so.' He resisted the temptation to state the obvious: that his claim went back a thousand years.

'You haven't forgotten the ice cream I promised, have you? I made two flavours.'

Rosie wasn't sure when she had decided to treat Don Xavier as a normal human being, rather than as an aristocrat with centuries of breeding behind him. They were wildly unequal in every sense, but, as nothing could change that, she had decided to be herself.

Maybe it was the Doña Anna effect, Rosie reflected as she reached for two bowls. In this one precious inheritance Doña Anna had made sure they were equals. The Spanish Grandee and the orphan housekeeper shared a huge responsibility thanks to the way that Doña Anna had drafted her will, but the more Rosie thought about it, the more it seemed to her that Don Xavier's need for an heir gave her some leverage over him. She had no other power to wield, but he had a schedule to meet, or he would forfeit his fifty per cent of the island to her. Of course, she could just wait him out and hope he couldn't produce an heir in the time specified, but she had no intention of wasting two years of her life hanging around for that. She wanted to get things moving on the island for the sake of the islanders as soon as she could.

Which, ideally, would mean working together, she thought, deflating somewhat when she caught sight of Don Xavier's unsmiling face.

Dipping down, she reached into the freezer to pull out the boxes of ice cream. The air in the kitchen seemed to have frozen harder than the ice cream in the tub.

Whatever happened next, she wasn't going to be

railroaded into making any decision that didn't feel right. She might have everything to learn about being a landowner, but Doña Anna had taught her not to be silent and accepting, but to question everything.

'Vanilla,' she announced, prising the lid off the tub. 'And Doña Anna's favourite—fresh strawberry. I picked the fruit from the garden this morning—'

'I haven't come here to eat ice cream,' the towering monument to privilege and wealth currently occupying her kitchen coldly stated.

He hadn't expected Rosie to be so relaxed on this second meeting, Xavier realised. She'd had time to think about things, and must surely realise the hopelessness of her situation. He was stationed at one end of the kitchen table, while she was at the other, and she didn't seem concerned at all. As she opened a drawer to reach for a serving spoon he put the documents he'd brought with him very prominently on the table.

She didn't look at them once—or didn't appear to, but then she baited him with a level stare. 'These look official,' she said, moving them out of the way so she could arrange her dishes. 'They look like the type of papers that won't bring anyone any happiness. "Beware of lawyers, " Doña Anna used to tell me. "Trust no one but yourself, Rosie." So…what flavour would you like?'

He was taken aback for a moment. He had dealt with many difficult situations in business, but nothing like this. 'What else did Doña Anna warn you about?'

'Honestly?' she said, pulling an attractive face as she thought about it for two seconds. 'Nothing. Not you. Not anything. I think she must have trusted me to get on with things. And at the end, when she was dying, and I knew I was about to lose the best friend I'd ever had, the last thing on my mind was lawyers, or wills.'

He believed her.

'I'll look at the documents later,' she said, 'if that's all right with you?'

And if it wasn't all right with him, she would still look at the documents later, he guessed. In fairness, nothing would bounce him into doing anything in a hurry, so he couldn't argue with that.

'There *is* one thing I feel compelled to do,' she said, 'and I hope you'll go along with me in this one little thing…'

'That depends what it is,' he said.

If they never did anything else together, they would do this, Rosie determined. The ceremony she had in mind held as much significance for her as toasting the life of a loved one in champagne at a wake. Taking a moment to celebrate the life of a very special woman, who had done so much for both of them, before normal hostilities were resumed shouldn't be too much to ask. It was time to find out.

'No ice cream for me, thank you.' Don Xavier put

up his hand as if to ward off the scoop of ice cream she was offering him.

Her stomach was clenching with apprehension, but she'd started so she'd finish. 'I'm afraid I must insist.'

'You must *insist*?' he said, scanning her face as if he thought she'd gone mad.

'I don't have any champagne to toast your aunt,' Rosie explained, 'and as Doña Anna loved ice cream, I thought we could both take a moment to remember her.'

Her throat was so tight by the time she'd finished this little speech she couldn't have argued with him if she'd tried, so it was a relief when he reached for the bowl. Lifting her own bowl, she proposed huskily, 'To Doña Anna…'

A muscle flexed in Don Xavier's jaw, and then—and she was sure she wasn't mistaken—the faintest hint of amusement sparked in his eyes. So he was human after all. 'I'm sure if we do this together, we can do more things together,' she prompted as she waited for him to start eating. She had to stop herself exclaiming with relief when his firm mouth closed around the spoon.

'Doña Anna,' he murmured, holding her gaze until heat flared inside her.

'Doña Anna,' she repeated, trying not to meet his eyes as she wondered what else he could do with that sexy mouth. He was just so unreasonably hot. She had never been alone with such a good-looking man before, let alone so close to him. Her ideal was based on the heroes in the books she used to read to Doña Anna, and they were all big and dark and dangerous too.

And that was quite enough rambling off-track for one day, Rosie warned herself firmly. If Don Xavier had made the slightest move she'd have run a mile.

'Are we done here?' he asked, dipping his head to bait her with his piercing stare.

'Yes, I think so. Thank you for that.' Her body thanked him very much. She was tingling with awareness.

He wanted to smear her with ice cream and lick it off slowly. He wanted to lay her down on the kitchen table and attend quite thoroughly to Señorita Clifton's every need. He wanted to explore every hungry part of her body slowly. He could certainly see some use for the ice cream. The contrast of heat and cold would be a torment to her—to him too, but that torment would end with pleasure so extreme, they would never forget it.

'The tour?' he prompted, shaking himself around.

'Of course.' She smiled primly into his eyes, but he couldn't help wondering what was going on behind that lambent gaze.

Why did the one woman in the world he needed to eject from his life as efficiently and quickly as possible have to be so desirable, and so ready for seduction?

Why did she have to be so infuriatingly in his way?

It was vital to keep his mind on his goal, which was to own one hundred per cent of the island. He had to leave all thoughts of seducing Rosie Clifton out of it.

'When we've completed the tour, you can sign the documents…' He glanced at them.

Her gaze followed his to the table. 'I'll have to read them first,' she said. 'That's another lesson Doña Anna taught me,' she explained blithely. 'Never write anything down that you're not happy for the whole world to read—and never sign anything until you know what you're putting your name to.'

Striding to the kitchen door to hide the impatience on his face, he opened it. 'Don't you trust me?'

'Should I?' She looked up candidly as he closed the door behind them both.

He should be used to her directness by now. She'd never had the chance to develop social niceties, he allowed. What you saw was what you got with Rosie Clifton. She had to be the most straightforward woman he'd ever met. 'Those documents concern the future of the island,' he informed her. 'Something I thought you cared deeply about.'

'I do,' she assured him, 'but I care for Doña Anna's last wishes equally.'

'In that case, you'll read them and sign them.'

'When I've read them, I'll decide what to do,' she said in a pleasant tone that made it hard to argue.

'We'll discuss it later,' he snapped. 'It's getting dark.'

Later? She kept her cool, but inwardly she quailed. How long did Don Xavier plan to stay? As for reading the documents later, she got the distinct impression that it didn't matter whether she did or not, as his decision regarding the island was already made.

'Do I have your attention, Señorita Clifton?'

'You have all of it,' she said honestly, running to catch up with him. She would have to be made of wood not to be impressed by his staggering good looks and his physique, but even they couldn't compete with the force of his personality. 'Shall I lead the way?' she suggested pleasantly.

'Would you?' he murmured, mocking her, she was sure.

'I'd love to,' she parried, guessing this might be the one and only time she got one step ahead of Don Xavier.

CHAPTER FIVE

THIS WAS WORSE than he'd thought. The tour took far
longer than he'd expected. So long, it was almost
dark by the time they had finished with the house.
How long had he been away from the island? He
hadn't thought it long enough for everything to fall
into ruin. His expression had remained carefully neu-
tral throughout, but both he and Rosie knew that if
he'd spared his aunt some time he could have stopped
the rot in its tracks. Things were so bad it would be
better to demolish the hacienda and then rebuild it.
Even here on the deck in the shadows of dusk he
could see the timbers were rotting beneath his feet.

Rosie watched him as he walked, brooding. Buy-
ing her out and then keeping her on to act as a link
between his team and the islanders had been one
possibility, but that possibility was gone now. She
might be well respected on the island, but the work
required was way beyond her scope to direct. He
had tried telling himself that this was just one more
business negotiation amongst many, but the agony on
Rosie's face when he uncovered each new flaw had

found a way past his defences. His expression alone must have told her that the house was beyond repair. It should be demolished before there was an accident.

At least he understood why Doña Anna had been so keen to keep him away. She had hated change, and must have closed her eyes to the deterioration. She had been fiercely proud, refusing all his offers of help. He had begged her to accept professional care when her health had begun to fail, and money for the island as well, but she had turned him down on both counts, insisting that the island was doing very well, thank you, and she would source her next companion from one of the many charities he funded. With the prince's prompting, Rosie Clifton had seemed the obvious choice. If he'd only known then how things would work out—

'Something wrong?' he called after Rosie, who was heading back inside the house at speed.

'I'm cold. I need a cardigan. Please…make yourself at—'

He heard the break in her voice, and guessed the blinkers were well and truly off. Seeing everything through his eyes had been an unwelcome wake-up call. Only a matter of days ago, he would have thought her tears a good thing. Of course she would cry. Of course the helpless little orphan would look to him to save the day, but the situation had turned out to be far more complicated than that. He understood property, and could take a realistic view. Rosie only knew that this was Doña Anna's home, and as such she thought the hacienda was inviolable.

At least she understood the enormity of the task now. She had no option but to sign the documents. She couldn't raise the money. She'd already tried, and failed. She had to accept that only his wealth could save the island. He was offering far more than her share was worth in recognition of her care of his aunt. But Rosie's job was done now, and it was time for her to move on. If she proved foolish and refused to take his money, his lawyers would take over. Whatever Rosie decided, the outcome would be the same. He wouldn't allow his judgement to be clouded by his growing interest in some young girl, and he had never entered into a negotiation without it ending in success for him. The only difference this time was some slight regret that Rosie's sunny optimism would move on, out of his life. That, and the thought of some other man putting his hands on her, which made his hackles rise. It was time to remind himself once and for all that Señorita Clifton had no place in his life.

She'd done the one thing she had vowed not to do, Rosie fretted, tense with frustration and anger because she'd shown her feelings; something she had learned not to do in the orphanage. Don Xavier had undone her control in a couple of hours. And now she had run away from a problem—several problems: the house, the island, her inheritance, and him. She was currently locked down in the sanctuary of her bedroom, trying to work out what to do next. It wasn't as if she had any experience in high level negotiations. During the tour, he'd found fault with everything. That hurt when this was the only home she'd ever known. But it didn't mean she was going to roll over and sell out. She had to find a way out of this, or squads of men in steel-capped boots would be marching over the islanders' carefully tended fields in no time flat. And, yes, the house was dilapidated. She was even prepared to believe it was as dangerous as he'd said, but both house and island deserved a second chance.

'What doesn't kill you makes you stronger,' Doña Anna used to say. She had to keep on with the regular meetings she'd set up with the islanders, and lobbying the big food chains until one of them came on board with her ideas. She wouldn't give up until the very last hope was extinguished. And when that light went out, she'd think of something else.

Sitting bolt upright on the bed, she stared up stubbornly at the damp patches on the ceiling to make a vow that Isla Del Rey would never become another of Don Xavier's flashy hotel schemes. She would fight on, as Doña Anna had done all her life. 'Whatever it takes,' the old lady used to say, 'we must keep the island authentic, Rosie.' And if Rosie had to keep Don Xavier in a headlock until he backed off, she'd somehow find the strength to do it.

She was gone so long he decided to go upstairs to choose a bedroom.

Preferably one with Señorita Clifton in it—

He killed that thought stone dead. He could afford

no distractions. The work here couldn't wait. He'd brought an overnight bag, guessing his inspection might take some time—

'Señorita Clifton!' He had almost barged into her as she came bowling out of her room. 'Are you all right?' he asked, steadying her. He could feel her tension as well as her fire beneath his hands. Her eyes were black with passion as she stared up at him.

'Don Xavier!' she flashed as if riding the crest of a wave of anger.

'What's eating you?' he said.

'Your plans to wreck the island, if you must know,' she flared.

Too many hormones; too few avenues for them to escape, he concluded as he huffed a short laugh. 'You obviously know more about my plans than I do.'

'So you deny that you're going to level the land and build another of your hotel schemes on the island?'

Her breasts were rising and falling rapidly as she sucked in air. She was a wild little animal, he thought as he stared down into her impassioned face. Curled up close in her burrow most of the time, she was a tigress when she set herself free.

'Nothing is decided yet, so may I suggest you calm down?'

'Don't patronise me. Calm down?' she derided. 'You'd better let me go,' she warned.

Yes. He better had. He'd been hanging on to her

all this time, and she hadn't exactly been fighting him off.

'I know you must be upset by what I've shown you today,' he said, trying for a reasoned tone, 'but I have a duty to point out the dangers when you're living in the house.'

Her eyes filled with tears. He didn't know what was worse, seeing her angry, or seeing her miserable.

Proud to the last, she whipped her face away from his.

'You've nothing to worry about,' he said, somehow overcome by a sense of how alone she was. It had to be because he was back in the old house, he reasoned as he continued to reassure her. 'I'll stay on until I've made a full inventory of the remedial work that needs to be done here.'

'What?' She turned a shocked face on his.

'You must have expected me to stay the night?'

'Actually, no.' Her stare was levelled on his. 'I'm surprised you're prepared to risk the danger.'

He tried so hard not to smile. 'I think I'm equal to the dangers here, Señorita Clifton.'

She stared at him defiantly as she braced her angry fists against his chest.

Lifting his hands, he let her go.

It took her a moment, but she was right back in the game within a couple of heartbeats. 'Of course you must stay the night,' she told him in a pleasant tone. 'This is as much your house as mine.'

He inclined his head, wondering how long her

warmth would remain imprinted on his hands. The memory of that small, soft body straining against his would stay with him for a long time.

He took the torture like a man. 'There are six or seven bedrooms, as I recall,' he observed in a matter-of-fact tone. 'Which means I can sleep at one end of the house, while you sleep at the other.'

'You won't trouble me,' she assured him.

He disagreed. He imagined that even with their doors locked and bolted, and at opposite ends of the house, they would trouble each other all through the night.

'I'll be right back with some clean linen for you,' she offered, hurrying away.

She could feel the heat of Xavier's stare on her back, and the moment she was out of sight she leaned back against the wall to grab some down time from the tension. What was happening to her? He was like a magnet drawing her into danger, and she had no more sense than to go with it. Worse, she didn't want to fend him off. His touch was light and unthreatening—she could still feel it on her arm. Closing her eyes, she enjoyed the sensation for a moment, but that only made her want more.

Her feelings were all over the place. She should hate him for what he represented, and for the danger he posed to the island with his schemes, but while hungry fire was surging through her veins that wasn't easy. And now he was going to stay the night. It was too intimate, too disturbing in every way. She would have preferred to keep him at arm's length—preferably with an arm as long as a continent.

Opening the door, she rifled through the linen closet, choosing the best of a bad lot in a pile of threadbare sheets. But at least they were clean and smelled of sunshine, she reassured herself, bringing the bedding to her face as she walked down the corridor. She could hear Don Xavier banging about in one of the rooms. She stopped outside the door, drew a deep breath, and then knocked politely.

'Come…'

His imperious tone made her blood boil. She was being hospitable, while he was treating her like a… like a housekeeper, Rosie thought, fighting back a laugh. That was exactly what she was—or what she had been. The humour in the situation soon restored her high spirits. Entering the room, she took in everything at a glance: his expensive leather bag and the crisp clean clothes arranged neatly on the bed…

And *him*.

So much *him* her heart was thundering like a jackhammer. Even now she couldn't get used to the sight of so much man.

'Señorita Clifton?'

Adopting a polite, yet remote expression, she laid the folded sheets on the bed.

'My apologies, *señorita*, I will move these things away, and then you can make up the bed for me.'

Judging by his raised brow, her jaw must have dropped to the floor.

'Do you have a problem with that?' he asked with surprise.

Yes. She did. She was going to start as she meant to go on. He had two hands just as she did. Even a little thing like making up his bed could give Don Xavier the wrong idea. As far as this inheritance went, they were equals. If she gave him the impression that nothing had changed and gave in to his every whim, how was she supposed to stand up against his plans for the island?

'You'd make the bed for a friend, or for a welcome visitor, wouldn't you?' he probed, identifying the problem right away.

'Gladly,' Rosie admitted, 'but as you have yet to prove that you're either of those things...'

His laugh cut her off. 'You're a source of constant amusement to me,' he admitted. 'I never know what to expect from you next.'

'Goodnight?' she suggested. Turning on her heels, she headed for the door.

'We'll continue our tour at six o'clock sharp.'

'It's barely light then—'

'It's light enough,' he ruled. 'I have many other things to do. I'm a very busy man, *señorita*. I can't hang around here for ever.'

Thank goodness.

'Goodnight,' he said.

As his firm mouth tugged in the suspicion of a smile, she shrugged. She'd been dismissed, Rosie gathered. She was careful to close the door behind her with barely a click, when the urge to slam it in Don Xavier's mocking face was overwhelming.

He was up well before dawn the next morning. He hadn't slept. He hoped Señorita Clifton had enjoyed a similarly disturbed night. He stared at his reflection in the mirror, furious to have her intrude on his thoughts first thing. All night, he conceded. She had been in his head all night.

If things had been different between them, their differences could have been settled in bed, but that wasn't an option with Rosie Clifton, who was so obviously enjoying giving him the runaround. She was testing her female power; something new to her, he suspected. When they'd first met she was uncertain, yet controlled, but now those amethyst eyes flashed fire at him on a regular basis. He liked that. He liked her. She was as fiercely determined as he was to see her plans through. She would make a worthy opponent in any dispute, which would make the pleasure, when she finally admitted defeat and accepted a settlement for her half of the island, all the sweeter. It would certainly please him to escape the parent trap his aunt had laid.

Okay. Stay cool, Rosie directed herself as Don Xavier came out of the house. If he'd been stunning in those cut-off shorts, he looked even better in banged-up denim that fitted snugly on his hips and, um, lower body…desert boots, and a close-fitting top that hinted at the muscular torso her memory could so readily supply. His inky-black hair was thick and tousled. His stubble was dense and sharp. He was dark and powerful, threatening and sexy in an immediate and very potent way. He looked as if someone had lit his blue touch paper this morning. But would she have the sense to stand back from the explosion?

'Good morning,' he called out.

Even his voice was virile.

'Good morning!' she responded brightly with what she hoped he would accept was an innocent smile. Did he remember how it felt to accidentally touch each other, or to hold her as he steadied her on her feet? Did he remember those glances between them that had held for several dangerous beats too long? Had he tossed and turned all night as she had? She could only hope—

'Ready for the tour?' he demanded, striding up to her.

'Absolutely,' she confirmed briskly. 'Shall we go?'

'Lead the way.'

As he drew alongside, her gaze brushed appreciatively over him again; once was never enough. It would have been so much safer to share her inheritance with a wizened old man, or even a pipe-and-slippers man, rather than this wild-haired brigand, who managed to look even more disreputable this morning than he had when he strode out of the sea.

She wished she'd tried a little harder with her own appearance, but lack of sleep and determination not to be late for the tour had led to her grabbing the first thing that came to hand, which happened to be an ancient top and even older shorts.

This isn't a fashion show, Rosie reminded herself, but just the start of some cold-blooded negotiations.

Really? Then, why was it so hard to concentrate?

Because she kept thinking back to Don Xavier taking his shower this morning. She'd been making coffee in the kitchen just a few feet below him when she heard the water running. She'd stilled, picturing him naked, his swarthy face turned up to the spray, eyes closed as he raked back his thick black hair. And then his lean, tanned hands moved on... slowly, down the length of his body, only pausing to map his iron buttocks, and a few other interesting landmarks on the way—

'Señorita Clifton?'

'I'm sorry...did I miss something?'

Blinking the erotic daydream away, she stared up into Xavier's shockingly handsome face. That didn't help her concentration either. 'Did you find the coffee I left on the stove?'

He frowned. 'I did. Thank you.'

'Good.' She was reluctant to leave those images in the shower behind, especially when he'd starred in her erotic fantasies all night.

'Is something wrong?' he asked when she bit her lip and frowned.

Only that it was time for her to get real. Don Xavier had only shown an interest in Rosie and the island when Doña Anna had given him no option.

'Nothing,' she said, knowing she must concentrate on the task in hand with a brain that had turned to mush from lack of sleep.

'I'd like to start with the path down to the beach.'

Xavier shot everything into sharp focus with just those few words. The path was narrow, and dangerously steep. There were loose rocks and shale where you could slip.

'This looks dangerous,' he said when they reached the top of the path.

If only he could see the island through her eyes—

'Hang on to me,' he insisted, offering her a steadying hand.

'It's fine. I go down here every day,' she said blithely, ignoring his help.

'If you come down here on your own, and you fall, you could lie here for hours,' he said. 'There should be a handrail, at least—'

She took big, reckless steps, just to prove a point.

'Wait!' he commanded, catching up with her. 'I don't want to be clearing up your mess if you fall onto the rocks.'

'I don't imagine you do,' she yelled back, slithering on regardless. 'How would that look in court?'

And then, somehow, he got in front of her. If she'd taken chances descending, he'd taken more. 'Take my hand,' he insisted coldly.

She ground her jaw and did as he asked. He showed no sign of moving otherwise. There was nothing cold about his hand; his grip was warm and firm, and left her breathless with mounting excitement. Until she remembered where they were and who he was.

'Watch where you put your feet,' he rapped.

Keeping them out of her mouth was her biggest problem.

'Tired already?' he demanded when she stopped halfway down.

'No. I'm admiring the view,' she said, refusing to make eye contact with a man who made her feel all sorts of unwanted things.

'You must have been impressed when you saw the coastline for the first time?' he observed in the most relaxed piece of conversation they'd shared.

'Seeing the beauty of the island after the city?' she said, feeling she should respond. 'You've got no idea.'

'I have some,' he argued, staring out to sea. 'I'm seeing things all over again.'

Thanks to her? Rosie wondered, watching the breeze ruffle Xavier's hair. No. She didn't flatter herself to that extent. Still, at least they were relaxing a little with each other, and that couldn't be a bad thing. 'After living in the orphanage, coming here was like visiting heaven on a day pass,' she admitted. 'I was startled by the island's beauty. Everywhere I turned, the vistas, the wide-open spaces, the freedom…' She stretched out her arms as if she could touch it. 'I couldn't see a single flaw—'

'And now?' he asked.

Her smile died. She hadn't seen a single flaw on the island until Xavier arrived.

'There really needs to be a proper handrail here,' he said as she continued her descent.

'There's no money for a handrail, not even for a rope.' She remembered how she'd begged Doña Anna to have something put in place, so the old lady could reach her beloved beach in safety. She could have kicked herself now, for not realising there was so little money in the pot. And guilty that she'd been given a wage at all, when that money would have been better spent on repairs.

'Did my aunt come down this path?' Xavier asked, frowning.

'Oh, yes,' Rosie confirmed, smiling as she remembered. 'She used to say she could slide down on her bottom, and climb up again on her hands and knees. "What's wrong with that, missy?"-she would ask me. Or, "Do you think I'm too old for that?"'

'And what did you say?' Xavier flashed her a look of genuine interest.

'I gave the expected reply, of course,' Rosie admitted wryly. 'I'd tell her that she certainly wasn't too old. But if I dared to venture an opinion—something like, "I just think—" she would cut me off mercilessly. "Don't think," she'd snap. "It's my job to think. Not yours."'

Xavier laughed. 'I guess we've both felt the sharp edge of her tongue.'

'I never took offence,' Rosie explained, enjoying the new warmth between them in spite of her wariness regarding Xavier's intentions towards the island. 'I just accepted that, however close we were, when it came to the Isla Del Rey, there was never any doubt that Doña Anna was in charge.'

And always had been until she died, but now the future of the island was up for grabs.

CHAPTER SIX

HE WAS DISAPPOINTED. Not because the island held any
surprises for him, but because he hadn't expected
it to be quite so run-down. The state of everything
stirred his nagging sense of guilt. He should have
come back long before now. He should have over-
ruled his aunt and done everything he could to make
her more comfortable, and see the island thrive. He'd
always been too busy, and she'd been adamant that he
must remain so. And now he knew why. She hadn't
wanted him to see that she'd lost her grip.

'The house has always been shabby,' he admitted
when he and Rosie reached the beach. Why he felt
the need to reassure her, he had no idea. 'Not that a
bit of peeling paint would have mattered to me when
I was a boy—I doubt I even noticed it.'

Slipping off her sandals, Rosie started to paddle
in the surf. She looked so young and so appealing
it was hard to remember that she was just another
hurdle in his way.

'You must have been glad of a home to come to,

after school,' she remarked, kicking the water so the spray caught the light.

'Doña Anna always made me welcome,' he agreed.

'And your parents?'

She had her back to him as she asked the question. She must have heard the rumours like everyone else. What Doña Anna hadn't told her, the islanders would have supplied. 'Best not mention them,' he said.

She turned to look at him and her mouth slanted attractively as she admitted, 'I have the same problem.'

He huffed a wry smile, but a spike of guilt stabbed him when he thought how much worse her childhood had been than his.

'So, what did you do on the island?' she asked, maybe trying to smooth over the awkward moment.

'I made a raft once out of driftwood just like this. Sadly, it disintegrated once I got out to sea.'

'Well, at least you didn't drown.' She laughed.

'Almost.'

'You should have made dens onshore. It's a lot safer.'

'Safety was never a consideration for me.'

'I guess that's why Doña Anna drove you out.'

'I don't blame her.' He laughed. He'd been a rebel through and through, but when he'd left the island he had tried to be a credit to his aunt. He'd thought that meant working as hard as he could to be the best, but even that wouldn't satisfy Doña Anna. She'd wanted an heir, a dynasty—

'What the—?' Rosie had splashed water at him, and now she was running away.

Choice: he could stand on his dignity, or he could give her a soaking.

As he caught up with Rosie and swung her into his arms he asked himself why his aunt had brought him back to the island and put a girl at his side like this—had she been determined to torment him from the grave?

As Rosie shrieked he dumped her in the sea. She shrieked even louder.

She recovered fast. Scooping up armfuls of seawater, she chucked it at him. He fought back. She gave as good as she got. She was so different from the sophisticated women he knew that he started to laugh, and laughing wasn't helpful when it came to winning water fights.

'How about I hold you under the waves for half an hour?' he threatened.

'How about you catch me first?' she countered.

And then she was off, like a dolphin, swimming effortlessly in her shorts and top. She could certainly swim. She might have grown up in the inner city, but she'd made up for it since coming to the island. Clambering out of the water, she stood dripping wet in front of him. Her outfit of choice was soaked through, the shorts so ragged, and the top so worn, he doubted even she knew what colour they had been originally. He thought he'd never seen anyone more beautiful.

This was really getting out of hand. 'We should go,' he said, bringing the high jinks to an abrupt end by turning his back on her.

He felt her disappointment follow him across the beach, and knew without doubt that he wanted her. Which was more than inconvenient. Lust was roaring through him, making nonsense of his agenda for the day.

Appointments could be postponed, he reasoned. He was under no pressure to leave the island right away. He could send for his people and have them come to him. It would be better for his team to see the island for themselves. He would set up his headquarters at the hacienda. It made perfect sense.

So much for keeping everything on a professional footing! Playing in the sea? Coming out of the water, looking like a contestant in a wet T-shirt contest with a see-through top clinging to her breasts? What was wrong with her? Was she crazy?

Xavier had kept his gaze confined to her face, but that smile playing around his sexy mouth said she believed he'd got the upper hand. She guessed he hadn't dumped too many of his sophisticated girlfriends in the sea—not that she was a girlfriend, or even close. At best, she was an irritation. So maybe the island had infected them both with *joie de vivre*—something else she guessed he wasn't used to.

When they got back to the house she had to admit

he was right about the improvements. Paint was peeling on the front door, and the timber around the windows was rotten. She supposed she should thank him for opening her eyes before the entire house fell on her head.

'After you,' he said, holding the front door open for her.

'Coffee?' she asked on impulse. 'Or are you in a hurry to get away?'

'You still have the documents to read.'

Trust him to remember. But she would take a look. He'd started to open up and so had she. It was the least she could do.

'But I'd love a coffee,' he added with a smile that warmed her through.

Was it too much to hope this ease between them could continue, and that maybe they could find some common ground that would enable them to work together for the good of the island? When they brushed against each other as they walked into the kitchen, it was just the lightest touch, but it might as well have been a lightning bolt to her overly responsive body. It was a reminder of how it had felt when he closed his arms around her to steady her. She had liked that feeling. A lot.

She made the coffee, and picked up the documents. 'I need to look at these alone,' she explained. Life and fantasy were becoming dangerously entangled. She'd lived on hope for most of her life, and was determined to be realistic now she had responsibilities. 'I'll call you when I'm ready. Why don't you take your coffee into the library?' she suggested. 'You'll be more comfortable in there.'

Was he listening? Xavier was staring at the kitchen ceiling, no doubt chalking up how many cracks there were, before moving on to assess the damp in the corners.

'Don't take too long,' he said, without sparing her a glance.

'I'll take as long as I need.' She meant it. He might exert a magical power over her body, but when it came to her promise to Doña Anna, nothing, not even Don Xavier Del Rio, could swerve her from her course.

'No,' Rosie announced from the doorway to the library where he was sitting. 'I'm sorry, but I can't accept this.'

He swung around in the library chair to stare at her. He'd been waiting in the library for over an hour. From the look on Rosie's face, they wouldn't be having a pleasant chat over coffee any time soon regarding money transfers from his bank to hers.

'I can't sign this. I'm sorry.' Walking deeper into the room, she put the documents on the library table in front of him.

'Then, what will you sign?' He stood to face her. He could understand her reluctance to accept so much money. She wouldn't know what to do with it. But he had advisors who could help her with that. Unless… 'If you don't think my offer's enough…'

'Your offer is an insult to someone who loved your aunt,' she argued quietly. 'If you had offered Doña Anna a fraction of that amount, she could have put everything to rights and you'd have no complaints about the island.'

'Are you asking for more?' He hadn't expected this, but Rosie had him over a barrel.

'I hope you're joking?' she flared. 'What you're offering is a ridiculous amount. You could buy a country for that. You've obviously got far too much money—'

He cut across her with an angry gesture. 'Then, what *do* you want?'

He hadn't achieved his level of success without taking every element of a deal into account. He'd seen other people fail when emotion was involved, which was yet another reason for him to remain exactly as he was. He would accept that there was no way of accurately calculating nostalgia in a monetary sense, but he'd done his very best.

'I want a say in the future of this island, and you're asking me to sell my right to that.'

'Correct,' he agreed. 'And my offer's fair.'

'No.' Rosie shook her head. 'I won't do it. I'm not thinking of me, but—'

'Doña Anna and the islanders?' he interrupted. 'Yes. I know your passion where they're concerned. But if you really want the best for them, you should leave the island to me.'

She huffed incredulously. 'Do you think there's even the slimmest chance of that?'

He shrugged. He'd up his offer if he had to. He did so, naming an amount that would make most people reach for a chair. Rosie didn't even blink. But then, it was as if all the emotion she had so successfully suppressed in life broke free. Snatching up the documents, she ripped them to shreds in front of his eyes.

'That's what I think of your offer!' she blazed.

Enraged, she was magnificent, but he remained focused on the deal. 'Everything has its price,' he said calmly.

'You still don't get it, do you?' she exclaimed, frowning with frustration. 'Even you don't have enough money to tempt me to sell my share of the island. You can't calculate everything in terms of money. When we were on the beach and you told me how much Doña Anna had done for you, and I told you I understood, because she'd done the same for me, I thought we were beginning to understand each other. But we're further apart than ever, because it's all about money for you. You don't care about the island. The only thing you care about is your bottom line. And winning,' she raged.

'That's easy for you to say—you don't have people depending on you for their jobs.'

'There's plenty of work on the island,' she argued.

'Growing vegetables?'

'Why not?' she blazed. 'What's more important—another golf club, or more food, good organic food?'

'Another of your little fantasies,' he suggested.

'If you would only agree to help the islanders with your connections, instead of driving on with your plan, I believe this island could be successful in every way.'

'Just as you believe you can live here with no visible means of support.'

'If I have to, I will.'

'But you don't have to,' he roared.

His tone shocked her. She had shocked herself. She was facing Xavier, braced for battle, when they were both usually so controlled. Somehow, combined, they were combustible. And now she couldn't stop. 'You can't buy the island, and you can't buy me!'

'Actually. I can,' he said with infuriating confidence.

She huffed incredulously 'You seriously think you can put a price on me?'

'I'm a businessman. That's what I do,' he countered.

'You're only a businessman thanks to the aunt you neglected—the aunt who gave you everything to help you become the man you are today. Do you think she'd be proud of you now?'

'I would think so, yes,' he said calmly, though niggling at the back of his mind was his aunt's unreasonable demand for him to provide an heir. What on earth had caused her to put that in her will?

His apparent composure rattled Rosie. It was as

if a dam had been breached and now a lifetime of suppressed passion came flooding out.

'I don't agree,' she snapped. 'Doña Anna expected more of you than this. I'm guessing that's why she gave me a say in her will.'

He could have told her that he'd sent regular payments to his aunt for years, but that she had distributed the money to the islanders, rather than keeping anything back for herself, but he was done trying to reason with Rosie Clifton.

Passion roared between them as she whirled around to stalk away. Catching hold of her, he brought her back. Cupping her face, he made her look at him, and then he finished the kiss he wished he'd started the night before. Rosie made angry sounds deep in her throat. He countered these with a lifetime of experience in seduction that only succeeded in making her madder still, but her lips were soft and warm, and he could be very persuasive. He had never felt such a desire to kiss a woman before, and within a few moments she was fighting to keep him close as animal instinct took over.

He wanted her. That was all he knew. He wanted her now—here on the library table. No waiting. No thought. Just sensation. Need and passion combined inside him, driving the primal urge to mate. His hands claimed her buttocks. He pressed her hard against his straining erection. She responded by throwing her head back, and groaning with need as she thrust her hips hungrily against his.

Fortunately for both of them, an alarm bell went off in some part of his brain. One of them had to show restraint. Unfortunately, as Rosie showed no sign of letting him go, that had to be him.

Her face was flushed with passion as he held her at a safe distance. Her eyes were as black as jet. She wiped the back of her hand across kiss-swollen lips, as if she couldn't believe what she'd done. 'My answer's still no,' she said.

He laughed. He couldn't help himself.

'You think this is funny?' she demanded in fury.

'Not in the least,' he admitted. He was impressed.

'I'm leaving,' she said.

'For good?'

'This isn't a joke, Xavier.'

He cut her off at the door. Planting his fist on the smooth wood above her head, he kept her trapped in front of him. 'My office will send the documents through again. May I suggest you sign them next time?'

'You're not listening to me,' she gritted out, meeting his unblinking stare fearlessly. 'I've no intention of signing your wretched documents.'

For just an instant he wanted to kiss her again. Then the wall he lived behind snapped back into place. It was time for Señorita Clifton to hear some hard truths. 'Your job here is done,' he said evenly. 'You need an income to live on, and that has to come from somewhere.'

'But not from you,' she said. 'Or do you think I'm incapable of earning a living?'

Pulling his fist from the wood, he stood clear of the door as she straightened her clothes and walked out.

Leaning back against the wall, he closed his eyes. Rosie Clifton was the most infuriating woman he'd ever met, but at least he now understood why his aunt had liked her—loved her, he amended. It had to be love that prompted such a generous bequest, unless his aunt's sole aim had been to torment him.

He decided not. His aunt had been spiky, but never vengeful. And Rosie Clifton's spirit had been forged under circumstances of extreme difficulty, which was why she had no trouble standing up to him. She might be naïve in many ways, but she was courageous and resilient. He guessed his aunt had seen something of herself as a young girl in Rosie.

'Xavier...'

He turned at the sound of Rosie's voice. She stood framed in the doorway. She had brushed her hair and washed her face. She looked a lot calmer.

'I came to say I'm sorry.' She lifted her chin. 'I haven't been very businesslike.'

'Neither of us has been very businesslike.'

'We were a little overheated,' she admitted carefully.

Putting it mildly, he thought. Even now he wanted her. He wanted to see that furious fire light again in his arms.

'I've been thinking how this place could look,' she said, glancing around, 'if I could persuade you to restore things, rather than to knock them down and rebuild. Maybe we could work together? I was angry before, after reading those documents, but I can't let my pride stand in the way of improvements.'

'And?' he prompted.

'And I've got a proposition for you.'

It had taken courage for her to come back and confront him. There was nothing to be gained by frightening her away—if anything could frighten Rosie Clifton. 'I'm listening,' he encouraged.

'It's not a long-term plan,' she explained, frowning as if the words wouldn't come easily. 'We'd have to see how it progressed year by year.'

'Not long term, then?' he observed dryly.

'I mean not permanent,' she said, refusing to be diverted from her thoughts with humour. 'With your money, and my understanding of the island and the people who live here, you could fund improvements, while I undertake the project management for you. I'd draw up proper accounts—'

As if that were all it entailed, he thought as she went on. Her intentions were good, but the island needed more than a few light touches, it required major renovation work, both to the house, and to the infrastructure. Architects and engineers—a whole raft of specialisms would have to be employed. 'All my projects are money-making schemes.'

'Then, you can afford one that isn't.'

'This sounds like a vanity project to me. You're asking me to pour my money into a house and island so that you can live here in comfort.'

'That's not it at all,' she argued, but her cheeks blazed red as it dawned on her that it must have sounded exactly like that to him.

'This island has to pay its way,' he said bluntly.

'I'm trying—and with your help and influence, maybe investors would listen to me.'

'As I have no previous experience or interest in farming, why would they?'

'So you'd stand in my way—when you weren't busy trying to find someone to give you an heir, that is.'

He was shocked that she would throw that in his face.

Xavier thought he held all the cards, but she wasn't even close to admitting defeat. She would find a solution to this. She had to.

'You should consider my proposal, Rosie. More money. You'd be secure for life. For the good of the island alone, you should accept it.'

But then she'd have all the money in the world to help the island, and no right to do so. 'My answer has to be no.'

There had to be a way out of the impasse. Doña Anna must have anticipated this situation, but what had she wanted Rosie to do? It was as if there was an unwritten message in the will, and she just wasn't getting it.

CHAPTER SEVEN

HIS TEAM ARRIVED that same afternoon. The dining room would serve as his boardroom for now. No one would stay overnight, so accommodation wasn't a problem, and the launch would take everyone back to the mainland.

Rosie was baking in the kitchen. She was up to her elbows in flour when he looked in. She had white smudges on her nose and cheeks, and added more with the back of her hand when she saw him.

'Ah, good, thank you,' he said, surprised and pleased at the effort she was going to on his behalf.

She frowned. 'Why?'

'Why what?' he asked, halfway out of the door.

'Why are you thanking me?'

'You anticipated my request,' he suggested with a shrug.

'Your request?' she queried, putting even more smudges of flour on her face.

He moved to one side as she moved past him to put her baking tray into the oven. She looked perfect for her role in the day ahead: casual, low-key, and efficient. His aunt would have tolerated nothing less. He found her very sexy in form-fitting jeans that clung lovingly to her curves. He lingered a moment as her simple white T-shirt rode up when she bent down, drawing his gaze to her soft, silky skin and the swell of her buttocks. 'Beautiful,' he murmured, temporarily distracted.

'The muffins?' she declared, straightening up. 'I'm using one of my all-time favourite recipes.'

The look she gave him when she planted flour-covered hands on her hips shot straight to his groin.

'Excuse me, please…' She drew herself in as she went to move past him, presumably so they didn't touch.

He stepped in her way. 'It's good of you to go to so much trouble for my team.'

'*Your* team?'

'The people in my team will really appreciate it.'

She frowned at him, confused. 'May I go now?' she murmured, still frowning.

'Of course.' He smiled as he stood back. 'Coffee would have been enough, though.'

'But cake's always nice, don't you think?'

His lips pressed down as he shrugged. 'If you insist.'

Remembering his colleagues in the next room, he turned to leave, but paused at the door to remind her to bring cream and milk when she served refreshments, and also decaf coffee for Margaret. 'A plate of biscuits on the side for those who don't like cake would be nice,' he added. 'Oh, and maybe a cheese sandwich to bridge the gap between meals. What are you serving later, by the way?'

There was a long moment of silence, and then she said, 'There must be some mistake. The muffins aren't for you. I can manage a packet of biscuits—'

'I'm sorry?'

'And I won't be serving meals, either, as I'll be busy later.'

'Busy? But you're the housekeeper.'

'I used to be the housekeeper,' she said. 'As you made clear, my job here is done. It ended when your aunt died. Only the bequest in Doña Anna's will allows me to stay on—that and my tiny pot of savings. As I promised your aunt, I'm not going anywhere. I'll be holding one of my regular meetings with the islanders today, so I can update them with where we are with applications and so forth. The cakes are for them. I'm sorry if you thought otherwise. If you'd asked, I'd have been happy to bake a double batch, but you didn't let me into your plans. That's why we need to work together.' She added, tongue in cheek, 'Perhaps we could cut them in half?'

'I take it that making coffee won't be beyond you?' he asked coolly.

'I'll leave everything you'll need ready on a tray, but I do have some chores I must do while the cakes are baking. Oh, and I'll need the dining room by four o'clock.' Seeing his expression, she added, 'Now you're back, we have to cooperate on certain things. I'm sure you don't want the islanders upset any more than I do, thinking everything's going to change overnight. They miss your aunt too. We owe it to them to keep things as smooth as possible. Cake will help,' she finished with a smile.

She might be young, and owning anything might be new to her, but she was learning fast. She was also sending him a message. This was not the young girl the lawyer had described to him, or the uncertain girl he had first met on the beach. This was a woman who was slowly becoming aware of the power she had been given, and who wasn't afraid to use it. He would have to rethink his plans where Rosie Clifton was concerned.

She had no complaints where Don Xavier was concerned. At least, not today. He and his team behaved perfectly, vacating the dining room at three-thirty prompt. They were to continue their discussions during a walking tour of the island, apparently. One of his team had even offered to stay behind to help Rosie in the kitchen.

'It won't take me long, honestly,' she told the kindly older woman called Margaret, who was a bit like a city version of Doña Anna, that was, a bit more put together, but with the same shrewd, wise air. 'I know you have to get away.'

Margaret wouldn't take no for an answer and picked up a clean linen cloth to dry the dishes. 'Don Xavier is an impatient man. I take it you've noticed?'

'I have,' Rosie confirmed as they shared a smile.

There was something in Margaret's eyes that said she was very fond of Xavier, and that any criticism she made was made with the warmth of a friend who knew him well. 'There'll be some changes here,' she said, glancing keenly at Rosie. 'You are prepared for that?'

'If I agree with them, yes.'

'You wouldn't want to see this place falling down, I imagine?' Margaret looked at her.

'Of course not, but I wouldn't like to see it bull-dozed, either.'

They cleared the kitchen together in silence for a while, then, folding her cloth, Margaret said, 'I know things seem black now, but remember you're still grieving. Both of you are. It should be possible to bend a little in time.'

'Really?' Rosie raised an amused brow. 'You see Xavier bending?'

'Give him a chance.' Margaret's soft tone held Rosie's attention. 'More importantly,' she said, 'give yourself a chance, Rosie.'

The rest of the afternoon was taken up with Rosie's meeting with the islanders, so she didn't have the time to think much about what Margaret had said. Her meetings were happy events, casual, but purposeful. Everyone brought something to eat in the break, and there was quite a feast laid out on the dining-room table. Don Xavier's team had left on the launch, so she thought it the ideal opportunity to ask him to join them. The islanders remembered him well, and she thought they'd be pleased to see him.

She was surprised by just how pleased. And this wasn't the aloof and arrogant man who had emerged from the surf like an invader come to claim his territory, but the man she had played with on the beach, a warm and engaging man amongst his friends. She doubted there'd be much time left for more formal discussion while so many reunions were under way, but that was okay. This was all she could have asked for.

Everything was going swimmingly until one of the elders of the village asked outright about changes that might be coming to the island.

'You have nothing to worry about,' Xavier told him before Rosie had chance to speak. 'My project will bring more jobs. Nothing will change for you. It will only get better.'

'That's not very specific,' Rosie tried to point out, but everyone was too busy smiling at Xavier and patting him on the back, telling him they knew he'd come back, and that he would never let them down.

He turned to look at her eventually, but it was the briefest glance. 'And you will have the reassurance of knowing that Señorita Clifton is here amongst you. You already know she has your best interests at heart.'

So everything was decided without a single word from her. But at least he'd accepted her staying on,

Rosie reasoned, so she'd hold back on confronting him right away. 'You still haven't told us about your plans,' she reminded him. 'Wouldn't this be a good time to share?'

'When the architect's scheme is finished, everyone here will be the first to see it,' he assured the room with a charming smile and an expansive gesture.

That went down well, but Rosie wasn't reassured. 'By that time whatever you decide to build on the island will be a *fait accompli*,' she pointed out.

She hated being railroaded, and as the conversation turned to dredging the bay to build a fabulous marina, and clearing vast swathes of land for the luxury hotel and golf course, she could feel her tension growing. Xavier could turn on the charisma, and had won everyone over. He could have suggested erecting a launch pad for moon rockets and she guessed the result would have been the same. Everyone was so pleased to see him, they would have agreed to anything he cared to suggest, and he would push these plans through, regardless of her opinion.

She waited until everyone had left before confronting him with her concerns. 'A six-star hotel? A golf course and marina? Do you think that's what Doña Anna intended?'

'Doña Anna isn't here to guard her island any more,' he said, easing onto one taut hip. 'We have to do that for her.'

She shook her head and laughed. 'You'll spoil the island. You'll tear it apart.'

'And you'd see it crumble into the sea,' he countered, straightening up. 'Improvements have to be made.'

'I agree,' she exclaimed with frustration. 'But why can't they happen slowly, and develop naturally?'

'You might have time for that—the islanders don't. I'm offering jobs today, not uncertainty tomorrow.'

And Margaret had said they could compromise?

'You only see what you want to see, Rosie,' Xavier insisted. 'And I understand why. You had a difficult life before you met Doña Anna. The contrast between here and the orphanage must have been extreme, so now you only see the good things and blank the rest. But that's no good to the islanders. They need progress now.'

'I'd do anything for them…*anything.*'

'I know that. So take my money. Make a good life for yourself,' he said quietly and intently, 'somewhere else.'

For a moment she was lost for words. The island was her home, the only home she wanted. It was everything she had ever dreamed of; that and a family of her own. The islanders and Doña Anna had given her that family, welcoming her to their beautiful island with open arms. Now it was her turn to do everything in her power to help them. She was getting better at writing to companies she'd found on the Internet, and she had sourced a huge number of charities to approach for grants. It was all work in progress, but she couldn't walk away from it now. Just because she hadn't received any positive replies yet, didn't mean she was ready to give up.

'Who is more likely to make things right for the islanders?' Xavier pressed. 'You, or me?'

His words stung her, because they were too dangerously close to the truth. But she couldn't back down now. She remembered the orphanage, and the matron deriding her. Rosie had wanted to stay on at school and go to college, but had been told that she could put that out of her head, as there were no funds for that sort of thing, and she didn't have the brains for it, anyway.

What if the matron was right?

Never mind that. Was she being selfish? Would Xavier's plans be better for the island?

No. Shaking her head, she remembered her promise. 'If you would only help me a little—maybe introduce me to some of your contacts, I could put the islanders' scheme in front of them, and try to get the business off the ground. Surely, there could be room for your scheme and theirs if everything was coordinated properly?'

'Are you backing down?'

'No,' she said firmly.

'In that case, I can only assume that you're asking me to help you fund your dream of Utopia.'

'All I'm asking is that you act as a go-between in this one small thing.'

'It isn't a small thing to invite my contacts to invest in you. Exactly how much experience of running a business shall I tell them you have? And make no mistake, Rosie, doing what you're suggesting—turning smallholders into commercial farmers—will be one hell of a business. You'd have to replace the infrastructure of the island, just for a start.'

'You'll need to do the same thing,' she protested. 'Why can't we work together?'

The sensible thing, Xavier reasoned, was to pay her off and send her packing, but so far they hadn't found a price. And though Rosie Clifton was the biggest risk to clear thinking he'd ever met, he was loath to send her away.

'If you're serious about this, you have to start thinking commercially. You need to meet the right people—'

'Exactly,' she interrupted, her eyes firing with passion. 'But how am I supposed to do that, unless you help me?'

'My money, your heart?' he mocked lightly.

'Why not?' She didn't even blink.

'All right,' he agreed, accepting her challenge. 'I'm holding a cocktail party at my apartment on the mainland. The guests will be exactly the type of people you need to meet.'

'Are you inviting me?' she asked him with suppressed excitement.

It was hardly fair of him to do so. His guests were hard-driven business professionals who would eat her alive.

'Are you?' she pressed.

'I'm not sure,' he admitted honestly.

'Why not?' she exclaimed.

'Because it might be said that every party needs a novelty item, an engaging piece of gossip to make it fly, and I'm not sure I'm ready to see you humiliated.'

'Only "not sure"?' she asked, starting to smile.

'I wouldn't stand for it,' he spelled out.

'I accept,' she said brightly.

Closing his eyes for a moment, he groaned inwardly at the thought of what Rosie's attendance at the drinks party would do to his precious clear thinking.

'All right,' he said. 'Decision made. You'll come to the mainland with me, and I'll do my best to make sure you don't feel out of place.'

She tipped her head to one side to stare at him with laughing eyes. 'You don't have much confidence in me, do you?'

The truth was, he didn't know what to expect from the redoubtable Rosie Clifton. But then she frowned. 'I don't know what I'm going to wear for this party of yours.'

'I'll buy you a dress,' he offered.

'I can't accept money from you—'

'*Dios*, Rosie! When are you going to stop being so proud? What are we talking about here—a dress and a pair of shoes? When you've sorted yourself out, you can pay me back.'

'When I've accepted your pay-off, do you mean?' she asked him suspiciously.

That was exactly what he meant. 'We'll think of something,' he said.

She had to accept. She was getting nowhere on her own, Rosie thought. And unless she could come up with funding for the islanders' scheme, Xavier and his team would steamroller his plans through.

'You think too much,' he said, reading her preoccupation. 'You want it—you've got it. Now, leave it alone.'

He was right. Building bridges between them was more important than worrying about her entry into high society. But...

'A cocktail party.' Her throat tightened on the unaccustomed phrase. 'I've never been to one of those before.'

'You've never owned half an island before,' Xavier pointed out, 'but you seem to be handling it.'

'Handling you, do you mean?'

He almost smiled. She did too. It was time for new beginnings. She had to take the next step, or he would leave her in his wake. She had to find the courage to finish what she'd started.

CHAPTER EIGHT

WHEN THE MASSIVE marble and gilt hotel where she was to stay on the mainland loomed into sight, Rosie thought it even more terrifying than the flight over from the island, and that had been something. She had never travelled in a private jet before. They used the bus at the orphanage, and she had caught the ferry to the island after flying there on a commercial jet with the comfort of hundreds of people around her. There had been no one to talk to or distract her in the hushed luxury of Xavier's private jet, as he had gone on ahead, and her nerves were shredded by the time the plane landed. The hotel was her second hurdle. The limousine that had brought her directly from the tarmac outside the jet had stopped outside the grand entrance. Her luggage would be brought up directly, the driver told her stiffly as she stepped out of the car.

Her throat dried as she mounted the marble steps and glanced up at the towering façade. Doors were opened before she had a chance to touch the handle, and once inside the lobby she found it bustling with elegant, beautifully dressed people, who seemed to smell of money; everything smelled of money to Rosie's untutored nose. There were huge floral displays, and such a mix of scents, sounds and new impressions they made her dizzy as she wove her way through the throng.

Having been given her instructions at the desk—where she'd stood in line for ages, only to discover she should have used another desk where they only handled those privileged individuals whose rooms were located on the higher floors—she crossed to the bank of elevators. Having tried frantically to operate the lift, she now discovered there was a man to do that for her. And the elevator cabin wasn't just a functional steel-and-glass method of moving between floors, but an elegant affair with a velvet banquette and gilt-framed mirrors. She was careful to stand well away from the walls in case she marked them.

'This is your floor,' the lift operator informed her.

'Thank you.' She'd had a chance to study her reflection. She looked so out of place it was almost funny. Except it wasn't, because she wanted to make the right impression, and, judging from the man's manner towards her, she hadn't made a very good start. He was probably wondering why Security had allowed her upstairs in the first place in her thrift-shop dress and worn canvas sneakers. She might have wondered the same thing, if she hadn't known by now that the name Don Xavier Del Rio opened any door. But whatever was waiting for her beyond the elevator doors, she would remember her promise to Doña Anna and hold her head up high.

She walked slowly down the subtly lit corridor, trying to take everything in. She felt as if she were wrapped in money, cosseted and protected from the outside world, which was obviously the hotel's objective. Even the air smelled expensive. And it was so quiet. The carpet was so thick it absorbed the sound of footsteps, while the walls were covered with silk rather than paper, which would muffle any sound. The décor was the type of tasteful opulence Rosie had only seen in magazines before. It must have taken a lot of putting together, she guessed, but it was certainly effective. Even the muted colours had been chosen to soothe the harried guests, providing them with a haven from their busy lives.

So what was she doing here?

It was time to put thoughts like that out of her mind. She had to think positively now. She was here to attend a cocktail party, whatever that might entail.

Her door was at the end of the corridor. After several failed attempts, she managed to get her key card to work. Standing on the threshold, she stared around. The room was so vast she couldn't take it in. Catching sight of her bedazzled expression in one of the mirrors on the wall, she quickly closed her mouth, closed the door—and then she saw the dress. It was spread out on the sofa with a soft cream wrap next to it. She loved the wrap, but her heart picked up pace when she took a closer look at the dress. It looked like something a starlet would wear. Cut to fit like a second skin, it had a plunging neckline, and a split up the side that would leave nothing to the imagination. No way could she wear underwear beneath it.

Picking it up, she walked over to the mirror and held it against her. The dress was obviously expensive and very beautiful, in its way, but if anyone had asked her honest opinion she would have said it was a bit flashy, and definitely not something she would have chosen for herself. She preferred to blend into the background, rather than stand out, and there was no hope of blending in a dress like this. With her shabby shoes and custard dress, she looked like a child about to dress up in her big sister's clothes. And then she saw the shoes lined up neatly on top of their box. But were they shoes, or instruments of torture? She'd never worn high-heeled shoes before. 'Pride must bear a pinch,' Doña Anna would have said. And she was being ungrateful, Rosie concluded, pulling a face. Putting her concerns to one side, she headed for the bathroom to shower and change.

'Do you want me to give you a hand?' Xavier's driver enquired politely when they had arrived outside what had to be the most impressive office building in the city.

'Would you mind?' Rosie had got herself stuck halfway between the car seat and the pavement. The dress was so tight, and her heels were so high, that she couldn't find a way of propelling herself forward, short of pulling her skirt above her knickers to free her legs.

'Just put your hand on my arm and trust me,' the chauffeur advised, 'and I'll get you out, somehow…'

He'd been quite stuffy up to that point, but now, when they shared a look at his suggestion, they both started to laugh. 'I'll take you inside,' he offered when he'd got her out in one piece and had steadied her on the pavement.

'Thanks for the offer, but I'll be fine.' She was terrified, but she had to do this on her own. She had to learn how big business and society worked if she was going to be any use to the islanders.

Did she want to learn how society worked?

Not particularly, Rosie concluded, when she was left on the wrong side of the revolving doors, while everyone else pushed past her, but Doña Anna had insisted that part of Rosie's development as a person must include broadening her horizons, so here she was, broadening them.

'Excuse me, please…' Pinning a confident smile to her face, she made sure that the next group approaching the entrance didn't brush her aside so easily, and finally she was inside the building.

The party was on the forty-fourth floor. She felt like a flamingo on stilts as she exited the elevator and followed the noise down the corridor. The double doors were open wide in welcome, while the room beyond was packed with elegantly dressed people, all of whom seemed to know each other. Breathing in, she begged pardon politely, and wove her way through the crowd towards Xavier. She had spotted him immediately. He was at the hub of everything. He was like a magnet that drew people to him. He was also the tallest and easily the best-looking man in the room, and her heart went crazy, though she determinedly blanked the fantasy of him turning to see her, and holding out his arms to embrace her, as if she were the only woman in the world.

He was busy talking and hadn't seen her arrive. She hovered in the background, listening. He was chatting about the island, saying he was keen to get started on his new scheme there, but there were one or two problems still standing in his way. The glances that passed between his guests made Rosie wonder if they thought she was the problem. A couple of the men turned round to look at her. Whether they recognised her from the newspapers, she couldn't be sure, but she felt uncomfortable when they started murmuring to their companions.

'Ah,' Xavier said, swinging around. 'Allow me to introduce Señorita Clifton.'

It was as if the entire room drew a collective breath. Everyone stilled and turned to look at her. She felt like a curiosity at a museum. Then, a man who was obviously important, judging by the way the crowd had parted for him, took hold of Xavier's arm and led him away, and the same people who had feigned interest in her only moments before now turned their backs on her and ignored her.

She stood for a moment, not knowing what to do. Her feet were killing her, and she was surrounded by a wall of backs. Kicking off the heels, she hung them from her wrist like a clumsy bracelet. She could probably have taken her clothes off too. No one would have noticed, but at least her feet were happy now.

She set off on a tour of the room, trying to engage people in conversation. They either ignored her or moved away. Determined that she would not be shut out, she grabbed a plate of canapés from the bar and started to offer them around. The plate was almost empty by the time she reached Xavier, and not one word of thanks had come her way. She had joined the ranks of invisible people, and vowed in that moment that she would never take anyone for granted, let alone ignore them.

Waiting politely until Xavier had finished his conversation, she waved the plate under his nose. 'Canapé, sir?'

'What on earth are you doing?' he said, frowning with surprise. 'And what on earth are you wearing?' he murmured.

'Well, you chose it.'

'I certainly did not.' He removed the plate from her hand and handed it to a waiter with a few words of thanks. 'One of the secretaries picked it up for you.'

How comforting to think she was like a file that

could be passed around the office for someone else to deal with.

Taking hold of her arm, Xavier steered her through the press of people to a cooler spot beside the door. 'Let's get out of here,' he said.

He took her to his private office. It was stylish, yet plain, with every gizmo known to man. She was impressed. She tensed as he closed the door, suspecting she'd let him down. She'd fallen at the first hurdle, making a hash of her so-called entry into society.

'Why didn't you introduce yourself around?' he said, frowning.

She had to laugh. 'You only have to enter a room and you're the centre of attention. I didn't know anyone here. More importantly, they didn't want to know me.'

Xavier's frown deepened. 'You should have said if you were having difficulties.'

'I wasn't *having difficulties*. I didn't want to interrupt your conversation, that's all. And these are your guests, not mine. I don't expect you to devote every waking minute to me.'

'Just a few of those minutes?' he suggested, slanting a smile.

She didn't like to think what that smile could do to her. And it was too late to blank it out. It had already warmed her, and reminded her of her favourite fantasy, that involved happy-ever-after with the man of her dreams. 'A few minutes would probably be enough,' she said.

Xavier sighed, and turned away as his smile broadened. 'I suppose I owe you an apology. I should have been a better host.'

'But it suits your purpose better if I leave empty-handed,' she said shrewdly.

He swung around. 'You're determined to think the worst of me.'

'Then give me a reason not to.'

The crease was back in his cheek. 'Maybe I will,' he said with a flash of his sexy dark eyes.

A few long moments, and then he laughed as he spotted the shoes hanging from her wrist. 'They didn't suit you?'

'They hurt,' she confessed.

'And you hate the dress—not a great result, clothes-wise.'

She plucked at the dress and frowned. 'I know it sounds ungrateful, but I have to agree, this is not my favourite outfit.'

Pulling his head back to stare at her, Xavier narrowed his eyes in speculation. 'How much do you hate the dress?'

'Well…' she tried to be objective '…it's obviously been designed for someone with far more sophistication than me.'

'That's very tactful. I think it was designed for someone who likes to be noticed.'

Well, he was right in thinking she had no desire to stand out.

'I don't like it much, either,' he said.

She shrugged. There wasn't much she could do about that.

But Xavier had an answer to just about everything. Taking hold of the dress at the neckline, he ripped it apart.

'How do you feel about it now?' he said.

CHAPTER NINE

THE BRUSH OF his hands against her breasts was a scintillating distraction, but it didn't take Rosie long to find her voice. 'There's a party going on outside this room,' she protested as she tried frantically to gather the ripped fabric together. She glared at Xavier. 'You're mad! There are people laughing and chatting on the other side of that door. Your guests!' she reminded him. 'Guests who could walk in here at any time and see us together! Like *this*!' she added, her voice rising at least another octave. 'You haven't even locked the door!'

Xavier's powerful shoulders eased in a relaxed shrug. 'That's half the fun.' His voice was low and confident.

'For you,' she argued. 'Who dares to criticise Don Xavier Del Rio? You can do what you want, when you want.' *And with whom you want*, Rosie silently added. Even she had fallen victim to his spell. She'd get nowhere until she woke up and seized back some control. 'The dress is ruined, and I don't have a spare tucked away in my evening bag, in case you were wondering.'

'I wasn't.'

He couldn't care less. She needed to work out how to walk back into the party with a dress hanging off her shoulders. It was time to man up and take control.

Well, that should be easy, she thought, fuming when she saw his mocking face.

Think—think... She wasn't going to allow him to pull her strings like a puppet all night, was she? It might not feel like it at the moment, but it was Xavier who was on the back foot. Her inheritance was safe. She could fight for the islanders for the rest of her life, and there wasn't a damn thing he could do about it. But he had to produce an heir. If she didn't make something of her advantage now, then she deserved to lose the island. Her mind raced through the limited possibilities. First on the agenda was sorting out her current predicament. Maybe there was a spare waitress's uniform she could borrow?

'So, Señorita Resourceful?' Xavier prompted with amusement. 'What are you going to do now?'

'More than you suppose,' she tossed back at him.

'Oh?' There was amusement in his eyes, but also a new wariness had crept in.

'You think you've got it all covered, don't you?' she said. 'You can walk out of here with a knowing smile, while I'm left to do the walk of shame into a party where I'm already unwelcome. I'm guessing you think this introduction to high society will put

me off for good, and that I'll be only too pleased—
grateful, even—to accept your pay-off, and go to live
quietly, while you move your bulldozers in.'

'You have an extremely vivid imagination, Señorita Clifton.'

'Do I? I think you see this as the start of returning things to how you imagine they should be,' she
said, still busily tucking and folding.

Xavier frowned. 'What do you mean by that?'

'You might even give me a job as a housekeeper
on the island, if I'm lucky,' Rosie said. Raising her
head, satisfied she had done the best she could with
the dress, she saw Xavier's jaw clench, suggesting
she was right. 'The Del Rio family will reign su-
preme once again, and everything in your world will
have returned to how it should be—in your eyes,'
she finished grimly.

'You know nothing about my family.' His tone
was ominously quiet.

'I can hardly believe you've got one. My theory is
that you were raised in a petri dish and then planted
on top of the gold at the end of the rainbow.'

'I have as much a family as you do,' he said.

'We both had Doña Anna,' she argued.

He was quiet for a moment, and then he shrugged.
'If you're upset about the dress, I'll buy you another.'

'The dress is the least of my worries. We can't
go on like this—you trying subtly, or not so subtly,
to drive me away. I'm. Not. Going. Anywhere,' she

spelled out. 'That's the last time I'm going to say it, so what are you going to do about that?'

Actually, Rosie thought, what was *she* going to do about it? Seizing control took more than good intentions. If she didn't like Xavier's suggestions regarding the future of the island, it was up to her to come up with something new.

'Take the dress off,' he murmured. 'It's ruined.'

'You're not listening to me, are you?' she demanded with frustration.

He smiled, and, though she knew she should stick rigidly to the point, those dark eyes held such danger they excited her. She wasn't used to flirting, and, though she knew this wasn't the time for it, the tension between them was threatening to snap. And then he made a big mistake. Putting a hand on her cheek, Xavier dipped his head as if to kiss her—as if it were his right! Don Xavier Del Rio had to learn that she could be dangerous too—

'*Que diablos*—'

Buttons bounced across the floor as she reached up and ripped his shirt apart.

She was filled with an unreasonable passion, born of the desire to assert herself. Why shouldn't she enjoy the heat of his hard, hot flesh beneath her fingers? Why shouldn't she lock her hands around what remained of his shirt and yank it apart? She was on fire. There was no chance of stopping her until both his shirt and jacket were on the floor. The fight was on. Xavier gave her no chance to enjoy her triumph.

Seizing what was left of her dress, he ripped it from neck to hem.

'What are you going to do about that?' he challenged as it fell to the floor.

Her answer was to launch herself at him. Pummelling her fists against his chest, she gave vent to her passion in animal sounds of anger that all too soon turned to sounds of need. When she had finally exhausted herself, and her blows had slowed, she looked up to find, to her frustration, that Xavier was still smiling. So much for seizing control!

'Why, Señorita Clifton,' he murmured, 'I would never have credited you with quite so much passion.'

She was breathing so heavily it was hard to argue, and the next thing she knew she was in his arms. Holding her firmly in place, Xavier cradled her breasts, and then chafed her nipples remorselessly until pleasure consumed her, wiping every sensible thought from her head. Dipping his head, he claimed her mouth, and with a thoroughness and skill that obliterated the world as she knew it. His kisses were addictive and he felt so unbelievably good. He tasted minty and hot, and, when she pressed her body against his, she loved the feel of his steel against her curves.

'Do you hate me as much as the dress?' he queried with amusement. 'I think you must,' he said, staring down. 'You lived such a quiet life on the island until I arrived.'

'I lived such a safe life,' she argued, but that only

made him laugh all the more. 'Don't,' she said, in between kisses. 'Don't make fun of me.'

'Is that what I'm doing?' he whispered, staring deep into her eyes. 'I thought I was making love to you.'

Cupping her face, he made her look at him, and, though she knew she should resist, she couldn't see anything but good humour and desire in his eyes. The first was unreasonably attractive, while the desire both terrified and excited her. He was tempting her to kiss him back. She didn't hate Xavier. She wanted him. She hadn't even known she was capable of feelings as strong as this. He nuzzled the exposed skin below her ear. The lightest touch of his sharp black stubble made her shiver with helpless need. Her body melted against his, while her breasts felt so full and heavy, and all she could think about was having him touch them again. He didn't disappoint her. Dipping his head, he lightly abraded the tip of each nipple with his teeth and with his tongue, until she couldn't deny him anything, and went willingly as he backed her towards the desk.

'It's the first time I've known you lost for words,' he commented with amusement as she gave a shaking groan.

'It's not my words I've lost, it's my dress. Aren't you even going to apologise?'

Xavier shrugged and his lips pressed down as he thought about it. 'I'm sorry,' he said, slipping his hand between her legs. 'Could you possibly ease your thighs apart?'

'That is not what I meant, and you know it,' she exclaimed on a gasp of shock.

'No, but it's what you want,' he said. 'So relax. Forget about the party and leave everything to me—'

She woke up like a shot. This encounter meant nothing to Xavier, but if she let him steamroller this too, her cause would be out of the window. She'd seen first-hand at the orphanage how destructive casual sex could be; someone always got hurt.

'Rosie? Rosie, what's wrong?'

Xavier's concern broke through to her. In his favour, he backed off the moment he felt her resistance, but now she was trapped in the past. Wiping a hand across her face, she tried to shake the ugliness out of her head. She must learn to move forward, and not become a victim of circumstance, which meant not doing something now she might live to regret.

The cocktail party was still in full swing outside the door. A tense silence had fallen inside the room. Then, an exuberant partygoer crashed into the door and the noise brought Rosie to her senses. 'What am I going to do about the dress?'

'There's a solution to every problem,' Xavier assured her.

'Even this one?' she queried sceptically.

'Of course.' Picking up the phone on his desk, he held her gaze as he pressed speed dial. 'Margaret? I'm in my study. I need you to do something for me.'

* * *

Margaret was a genius. She handed a shirt through the door, and made no comment when Xavier left the room to join his guests.

'I brought some dresses for you,' she called out to Rosie.

'Come in,' Rosie invited warmly, having kicked her ruined clothes beneath the desk. Luckily, some interior decorator had thought a fine cashmere throw would look amazing on one of the sofas and she was using it as a cover-up, so there was no embarrassment—well, not much on her side, and even less on the unshockable Margaret's side.

Once the door was safely closed behind her, Margaret held up the selection of dresses for Rosie to choose from.

'I can't thank you enough,' Rosie exclaimed with relief.

'I'm only sorry it took so long. Problems are my speciality, but miracles take a little longer.' Margaret eyed Rosie keenly. 'Xavier said you spilt something down the front of your dress?' She didn't wait for an answer. 'So I took the liberty of bringing underwear along as well.' She plonked down the boxes she had stuffed beneath her arm. 'Hope I got your size right. All I had to go on was our meeting on the island, and again tonight when you walked into the room.'

'I'm just so grateful, I'd grovel for a hessian sack tied with a piece of rope, but these are amazing. Thank you. It saves sneaking away wrapped in a throw.'

'I can't imagine you sneaking anywhere,' Margaret said frankly.

'I don't know what I'd have done without you.'

'Nonsense,' Margaret insisted. 'You would have walked through that door with your head held high, and to hell with what anyone thought.'

Rosie grinned. 'You're probably right.'

'That little red number hit the bin, I imagine?' Margaret said, looking at her shrewdly.

'You saw it?'

They both laughed.

'I would have come to your rescue sooner at the party,' Margaret explained with a rueful grimace. 'I could see how rude people were being to you, but I was talking to the ambassador at the time, and he's one person I can't ditch.'

'Please don't apologise. You've done enough for me as it is.'

'Of course I must apologise,' Margaret insisted. 'One of us should. Xavier's guests have behaved appallingly tonight, and he shouldn't have allowed it to happen. And I shall tell him so—'

'Please don't.'

'Well, at least let me make up for your rocky start to the evening,' Margaret insisted. 'When you're ready, I'll be only too happy to introduce you around.'

'You're very kind.'

'I'm very practical,' Margaret argued. 'As are you, Rosie Clifton. Ten minutes? Don't worry. I'll come back,' she said, heading for the door. 'Just call me when you're ready.' She glanced at the phone on the desk.

'Now I understand why Xavier has you on speed dial,' Rosie said, smiling at her new friend.

'I do have my uses,' Margaret agreed, shooting Rosie a brief, ironic look.

CHAPTER TEN

AFTER AN INTERESTING start to the evening, his party was deemed an unqualified success. Rosie had impressed him. She had moved with increasing confidence amongst his guests since Margaret had introduced her around. She looked stunning in an ice-blue dress cut on remarkably similar lines to her old yellow dress, though in some expensive designer fabric. Margaret had excelled herself as usual. The expression on Margaret's face at this moment, however, did not bode well. She was sailing towards him like a galleon in full sail. Taking hold of his elbow, she ushered him out of hearing of the other guests. He didn't complain. So long as he could still see Rosie, whatever Margaret wanted to say was fine by him.

'She's a diamond, that one.'

'You like Rosie Clifton?'

'Yes, I do. And you've treated her abominably tonight.'

'Is that what she told you?'

'Far from it,' Margaret admitted. 'She thinks you're wonderful, which just goes to show how mistaken a person can be.'

'I didn't ask you here to give me a lecture,' he chastised Margaret warmly, delighted to hear Rosie's opinion of him.

'You invited that poor girl, and then you left her stranded with people she didn't know. That's not good, Xavier. It's not worthy of you, and you know I'll speak my mind if I think you've done something wrong.'

'That's why I hired you,' he commented dryly.

'Then make it up to her. I've told her you'll see her safely home tonight. She wasn't happy about that, either,' Margaret conceded, avoiding his interested stare. 'But I'm sure you'll find a way to make amends.'

He was too.

'Use your powers of persuasion, if you want her to cooperate when it comes to the island,' Margaret suggested, as if he needed a prompt. 'Don't try and pressure her, or she'll fight back. She deserves better than that,' she added, directing a level stare into his eyes.

Having delivered her rebuke, Margaret sailed off in search of more wrongs to right.

'Who's taking you home tonight?' he asked, walking up to Rosie as she stood waiting to collect her wrap from the temporary cloakroom.

'You are, apparently,' she said, giving him one of her looks. She reserved her smile for the man who'd found her wrap, he noticed.

'You're very forward, Ms Clifton.'

'I'm very forward? You have a lot of ground to make up for tonight. If Margaret hadn't intervened, I'd be calling a cab back to the hotel right now.'

'It would be my pleasure to take you home.'

'Thank you,' she said coolly. 'Margaret said I must be sure not to leave without you.'

'She makes me sound like an umbrella.'

'Slightly more ornamental,' Rosie commented as she turned to thank the cloakroom attendant.

'Thank you,' she said primly as he stepped forward to help with her wrap. His only reward was the way she trembled when his hand touched her naked skin as he lifted her hair out of the way.

He stood back to watch as she walked to the exit. A couple of his guests stopped her to say goodnight, and to press business cards into her hands, and one of them was the ambassador. She'd been a hit tonight.

He arrived at her side in time to hear the elderly statesman purring over her hand, 'It's been a pleasure meeting you, Señorita Clifton.'

He guided her away from the ambassador with a few polite words, as well as all the other men standing in line to say one last goodnight to the very attractive Rosie Clifton.

'I think he's nice,' she said as he led her away. 'Are you jealous, Don Xavier?'

He huffed a dismissive laugh. 'I have to agree, you do look rather young and innocent in that dress.'

'Because I am young and innocent,' she reminded him with no smile. 'But that doesn't make me naïve, except where business is concerned, and there I'm happy to admit that I have everything to learn—with your help,' she added, with a flash of her astonishing eyes.

'So I'm on board with *your* plans now, am I?' he queried with a quirk of his brow.

'I don't know. Are you?' she said.

He chose not to answer and called for the lift. Rosie wasn't afraid to speak her mind, and in that she had joined a very exclusive group of women, consisting only of Margaret, and his late aunt, Doña Anna.

He drove her home. To his home. One of several he owned in the city.

'This isn't the hotel,' she commented.

'Well spotted,' he said dryly, noting the fact that her bravado was fast leaching away. He drove in through the gates. The mansion overlooked the park, and was both vast and beautiful. He was very proud of it, and found himself hoping that she liked it too.

'So why have you brought me here?' she demanded.

'For a nightcap?'

That half-serious suggestion was met by another piercing Rosie look. 'A nightcap?' she repeated sceptically. 'You know I hardly drink.'

'Neither do I, but I thought it would be a chance for us to get to know each other better.'

'Something Margaret suggested you should do?'

He pulled his luxury sports car alongside the steps. 'I do have some original thoughts. Let's call it a peace mission. One drink,' he said.

'And then I'm leaving,' she confirmed.

He helped her out of the car, and took her straight inside to the library, where his staff had lit a blazing fire. She looked around with interest. This was his favourite room in the house, and, for some reason, it really mattered to him that she liked it. The furnishings were comfortable and the walls were lined with books. Just the smell of old paper and worn leather bindings soothed him, and he definitely needed something to soothe his raging libido. Their clashes at the drinks party had taught him a lot about Rosie Clifton, and had confirmed his belief that fierce fires raged beneath her cool exterior, which wasn't helping his sexual hunger at all.

She might be out of her depth and sinking fast, but Rosie had to rally and stand up to him. Why had Xavier brought her to his fabulous home? Did he think he was going to seduce her? No chance. Still, this introduction to his luxury lifestyle told her more about his huge wealth and impeccable taste than the media could ever hope to with a few photographs and a lot of hysterical guff. She'd had so many new experiences tonight, her head was reeling, but she would sort it out. It didn't help that her body was on full alert after that encounter with Xavier's erotic expertise, but she would tame that too.

'You like the books,' Xavier commented as she allowed her fingertip to drift across a row of what were almost certainly first editions.

Discussing such a harmless shared interest gave her calm time, thinking time. 'I love them.' She had never seen so many leather-bound volumes gathered together in one place before. 'How can you ever bear to leave this house?'

He shrugged. 'I have books in all my houses.'

'Lucky you,' she murmured as she walked along the line of books. So many of the stories she'd read to Doña Anna had involved an unequal partnership, but that hadn't stopped the heroine succeeding— sometimes with audacity, but always with courage. An idea had been banging around in Rosie's head since their encounter in his office. It was radical, but might just work. 'Reading was the first thing that brought me close to your aunt.'

As he hummed she sensed she'd struck a nerve. It was perhaps better not to mention anything about her relationship with Doña Anna while things between them were still strained. 'Why did you ask me here?' she said instead, moving away from the books to face him.

'I'm trying to make amends.'

She didn't believe him for a minute, especially as he was opening a bottle of champagne.

'You do drink champagne, I take it?' he said, catching her look.

'I don't know,' she admitted honestly. 'I've never drunk champagne, but I'd love to try a small glass.'

A flash of surprise crossed Xavier's face. She guessed there were a lot of things he took for granted that she had never tried. 'But there's never been a better time for champagne.' Her heart started thumping as she got ready to spring her surprise.

'Oh?' he pressed with interest as he poured the foaming liquid into matching crystal flutes.

'Yes.' The prospect of voicing her solution to their problems was alarming, and if there had been any other way she would have taken it. But she had to be both courageous and bold, or she might as well pack her bags and leave the islanders to fend for themselves.

Xavier handed her a flute, which she eyed curiously. 'Would you prefer something else?'

'No. This is perfect. Thank you.'

This had to be what Doña Anna had intended all along, Rosie concluded as she reviewed her plan. She would be in charge of her own destiny, and she would have an equal say over the future of the island. Xavier had tried to buy her off, and when that failed he was trying his best to charm her, but she was the one with the leverage, not him. He was the one in need of an heir, and all the champagne and blarney in the world couldn't change that.

'Would you mind if I proposed the toast?' she suggested.

He frowned a little, as well he might—he would have run for the hills if he'd known what she had in mind. And she wasn't in a much better state. Her breathing had sped up. Her heart was beating so fast and loud she was sure he could hear it. This was huge, and once she spoke the words out loud—if, *if* he agreed, the die was set.

'Of course—go ahead,' he said indulgently, not suspecting for a moment what she had in mind. 'You've had a bit of practice, after all—the ice cream,' he reminded her. 'Well? What's your toast?'

She took a deep breath and then just spat it out. 'I think we should get married.'

Xavier's eyes widened. 'I beg your pardon?' he said faintly. 'Am I imagining things, or did you just propose marriage?'

'That's exactly what I said,' she confirmed.

He looked incredulous.

'It would solve all our problems,' she said. 'Yours especially,' she hurried on, 'so it seems to me to be the sensible thing to do—'

'Sensible?' His expression was incredulous as he raked his hair.

'Yes—shall we sit down?' she suggested. 'There are quite a lot of things to discuss.'

'You don't say?'

The look on Xavier's face suggested the world and everything in it had gone mad. He must be shocked, Rosie reasoned as she crossed the room to sit on the sofa.

'Please,' she said, injecting her voice with what she hoped was the correct amount of supplication. 'Won't you join me?'

Xavier's face was a grim mask when he came to sit across from her. 'Go on,' he prompted with a wave of his hand.

'You need an heir or you'll lose your half of the island to me, and unless you've got someone in mind—'

'I don't.'

'Then...'

'Better the devil I know?' he suggested grimly.

'You can't buy me out, you should know that by now, and if we marry you get to keep your share.'

'What's in it for you?'

'Everything,' she said bluntly. And nothing, she thought. 'A secure future for the island,' she went on. 'We can't leave the islanders wondering if they have a future with you, or with me. They need certainty, as I think you pointed out. And how can you risk your investment without that same guarantee?'

This wasn't the romantic marriage proposal she had imagined as a child. This was a cold-blooded transaction of a type that was Xavier's speciality. She hoped it would appeal to his logical mind. She had no hope at all that it would appeal to his romantic nature, as he didn't have one.

'Marriage would put us on equal footing,' she explained, 'and it would open doors that have been slammed in my face. I'd be able to help the islanders— really help them. You've seen how people react to me. No one wanted to speak to me at the party unless you were at my side, or Margaret was introducing me around. This would give me credibility, an equal say in what happens to the island, and it would give you the heir you need to keep the island.' Her stomach tightened on the words. The thought of sex with Xavier was the most terrifying prospect, but as she had so far failed to find an alternative—

'I can see that it would help you,' he said coldly.

'And you,' she insisted, ignoring the chill in his eyes. 'So, will you consider my suggestion?'

She had no idea what Xavier was thinking as he stared into the fire. Her best guess was that this was Xavier the businessman, weighing up the odds.

'I can't believe you're serious about this,' he said, looking round at last.

'You'd have my full cooperation,' she stressed, sensing the faintest of possibilities that he might say yes.

'I would certainly expect your cooperation in bed.'

Her heart clenched tight.

'I have a rather tight schedule to meet.'

It lurched, but she held her nerve. 'I hope we'd work together in every way.'

'I'd make sure of it,' he said without a scrap of warmth.

It was time to close the deal. She knew nothing about such things, and was firing on instinct. She surprised herself with how unemotional she could be when so much was at stake. 'This is for both of us,' she said levelly. 'Without marriage to me, the risk of losing your inheritance is very real for you, and I know the island means a lot to you, in spite of what you say. Isla Del Rey is as special to you as it is to me. You might have all the power and influence in the world, but without my cooperation in this one thing, your plans are stalled.'

'What do you know of marriage? Very little, I think,' he went on without waiting for her to answer. 'Marriage brings nothing but unhappiness. Wedlock is well named, in case you didn't know. People enter into marriage with expectations—or, in your case, dreams—and when they find it can never match up to these fictions, what follows is misery for all concerned.'

'In your case, maybe,' she protested.

'Can you quote a single instance where I'm wrong?' Xavier demanded. 'No. I didn't think so. You don't have a clue. And as for this heir Doña Anna has insisted I must provide. My aunt has gone down in my estimation. I would have thought that she, of all people, would understand that having a child in the middle of a loveless marriage denies that child the right to happiness, and that it colours the rest of their life.'

'Only if they allow it to,' she said, sensing Xavier was talking about himself.

'And what would you know about it, when you have no experience of relationships—none at all.'

'Except with your aunt,' she said steadily. 'And whatever you think of me, or Doña Anna, I will not break my promise to keep her island safe. And, yes, you're right in saying I don't have any experience of marriage, or happy-ever-after. I didn't have any experience of love until I came to the island and met Doña Anna, but one thing you must know with absolute certainty is that if I have a child I will love that child with all my heart, and I will never abandon it as you were abandoned. You need an heir, but you're sure you'll fail as a father, as you were failed by your parents, but why would that happen?'

'You're so sure of everything,' he said.

'Yes, I am. I have to be. I've had to be positive, or I'd still be back in the institution. Just think how you're loved on the island, and the love that's waiting for that child. Everyone hopes you'll return to Isla Del Rey one day, and that hope has no strings attached, or documents to sign, and nothing to be gained by the islanders, other than the rightness of you being back amongst people who love you. And I'll tell you something else—'

'I'm sure you will,' he said.

'You won't deny me my dreams, because I won't let you.'

'The hearts and flowers you imagine are not a given,' he said. 'I think you have a very naïve view of things.'

'Maybe,' Rosie agreed, 'but better that than I remain bitter about a past I cannot change. If we work together we could achieve a lot on the island. That's what I think Doña Anna wanted when she drew up her will. My heart, your business acumen,' she said, smiling encouragement. 'And, who knows? I'm sure we'll annoy the heck out of each other, but we might even start enjoying it.'

His cynical expression didn't promise that, but everything was on the line now: her heart, her fears, her future. 'This really matters to me, Xavier.'

'I'm sure it does,' he said, staring at her without warmth. 'Dipping a hand into my bank account would matter to most people.'

Shaking her head, she laughed, but it was a sad sound, totally lacking in humour. 'You haven't listened to a word I've said. This isn't about money.' *You infuriating, damaged man*, she thought. Xavier didn't think he needed help from anyone. He didn't need an island. He *was* the island, isolated and alone.

'One minute you're working in the orphanage,' he said, his eyes dark with suspicion, 'and the next you're inheriting half an island. And now you seem to think you can marry the other half.' With a shake of his head, he gave her a cutting look. 'Your idea of marriage might catch on. It seems like a very good bargain to me—for you, and for every other penniless woman in the world.'

'Then refuse me,' she challenged. 'I'm sure you'll

find someone to oblige you with an heir, with all that money at your disposal.'

Xavier's expression darkened. 'What did you imagine when you were offered the position of housekeeper to an elderly woman? Did you think it would give you the chance to charm my aunt into leaving you something in her will?'

'I think all you see is bad in people,' she countered, 'and I think that's sad. You're the loser,' she added heatedly. 'No wonder you're still alone. I'm doing this for the good of the island, and that's my only reason. Do you think that anyone would want to marry a man who can't feel anything, without a very good reason for it? And as for playing your aunt? I was stunned by Doña Anna's generosity. I still am. And I'm determined to do everything she expected of me. I will never forget how much I owe her—and I'm not talking about the bequest now, but the home she gave me, and the love we shared. I don't think my plan's naïve. It's not as if we're talking about a love match. Ours will be more of a business deal.' Her heart sagged as she said this, but it was done now, and she had to get through to him somehow.

'I think I know a little more about business deals than you.'

She shrugged. 'Then you must see the good sense in this. Work with me to put the island right.'

'Turn it into a vegetable plot?' he suggested.

She ignored that comment. 'Once everything is on an even keel, we can arrange a discreet divorce.'

'No stone left unturned,' Xavier observed. 'I'm impressed.'

And patronising, she thought. 'It's said your success rests on your ability to put plans into action right away—'

'Sensible plans,' he interrupted, 'plans that have been thoroughly researched, and will work. I can see what you have to gain from this—'

'And you,' she countered firmly.

'You're quite a hard little piece, aren't you?' he remarked with an accusing stare.

Not at all. Not even slightly, and she wilted inwardly at Xavier's description, though not a jot of that showed on her face. Living in an institution was a strange and enclosed experience. She couldn't have survived it without a little steel in her backbone—

Without a lot of steel in her backbone, Rosie amended.

'So, what's your answer?' she pressed.

CHAPTER ELEVEN

Doña Anna had tied him up in knots, ensuring he came back to the island, met Rosie, and then fulfilled his aunt's request to provide an heir. How neat. Doña Anna was the only woman in the world who had ever been able to put a curb on him. She'd done it once before when he was a youth, and she was doing it again from the grave. That Rosie Clifton had chosen to make this proposal, shocking him with her accusations, only endorsed his aunt's opinion of the girl. Whatever his answer, he had to admit his aunt had made a good choice in her lieutenant. He supposed he owed Rosie some grudging respect for the fact that she never gave up. Nothing would deter her from following his aunt's wishes to the letter.

'Marriage to you will give me the power to help the island,' she told him now, her face shining with good intentions.

'I'm expected to fund your ideas?'

'Only if you agree.' Her eyes were full of hope.

'This marriage to me will certainly allow you to continue your meteoric rise in the world.'

'Please don't talk like that when there's a child involved,' she begged him.

'*You* should remember that there's a child involved,' he fired back. He'd seen the effect of a marriage and a child on his parents. 'You do realise this would have to be a marriage in the fullest sense.' With consequences he dreaded more than Rosie, he suspected. Everything was fantasy and theory to Rosie, but now she must face the truth.

'Of course,' she assured him, but her face was ashen. He guessed she was thinking about their wedding night and all the nights after that.

'And if you expect me to consult with you concerning my plans for the island—'

'I do expect consultation between us,' she stated firmly.

Even as she spoke the words Rosie knew they were wasted on Xavier. He'd probably never consulted with anyone in his life. So maybe that was one thing she was better at than him, she reasoned. Her life had been one long series of negotiations, with compromise the only way to survive the system she'd grown up in. 'You might find it stimulating to hear new ideas,' she suggested.

'I have a team for that,' he said. 'But if we do run out of ideas, I'll be sure to call on you.'

'So your answer's no?' It was a struggle to read him as he stared into the middle distance.

'Not necessarily.'

Rosie had given him everything he needed on a plate. He was sorry she'd be hurt—and she would get hurt—but it couldn't be helped. His aunt should have known that this would have a bad ending. He'd never made any secret of the fact that the chains of domesticity were not for him. 'Yours is a very unusual proposition.'

'It's bold,' she argued.

'It's a marriage of convenience.'

'Yes,' she agreed. 'That's what's so good about it—both sides benefit.'

Was she being so businesslike because she thought it was the only way to communicate with him, or did she have that hard streak beneath her vulnerable shell? Looking at her face, he decided she was certainly gritty and determined. She was a survivor, like him, he concluded. 'Isn't a marriage of convenience a little outdated?'

'In this instance, it will be perfectly in tune with our needs.'

'Then I agree,' he said.

'You do?' She looked at him with surprise.

'Pay attention, Ms Clifton. I just agreed to marry you. As you so rightly say, my aunt has faced us both with a problem, and the best way to solve that problem is with a straightforward business deal. I agree that we should be married—and as soon as possible.'

Triumph came in many forms, Rosie now discovered. She felt light-headed in victory, and frightened at what she'd done. Her erotic fantasies involving Xavier belonged in her fantasy world, where he was everything she wanted him to be, and he made no unreasonable demands on her. In reality, he was too much of what she wanted, and his demands would probably be many and vigorous, but, with everything at stake, what choice did she have?

'Okay,' she said, extending her hand for him to shake on the deal. 'Let's do it.'

'You do know that in those few words your world has changed for ever?' he asked as he closed his hand around hers.

'I know it,' she whispered, sensation streaming through her at his touch. 'And I'd hoped my world would change,' she added levelly. 'It would have to, to embrace yours.'

'Good.' He seemed pleased. 'I'll have my people make a formal announcement. We'll have to celebrate. I'll hold a ball.'

'A ball?' Rosie was aghast. The drinks party had been bad enough. This was all moving too fast.

'It's usual to make a formal announcement,' Xavier assured her. 'We must give everyone chance to congratulate the happy couple.'

What happy couple? Rosie thought, shivering inwardly.

'Is something wrong?' Xavier asked her.

He knew very well what was wrong. She needed reassurance that she was doing the right thing, and there was no one, absolutely no one, who could give her that. 'I'm surprised you care what the world thinks about our forthcoming marriage.'

'I don't, but I thought you might,' he said.

She appreciated his concern. 'Thank you.'

'Don't mention it.' His stare was dark and triumphant, and it stripped away her brief moment of confidence, but she had to do this. It was the only way she could stop the island being torn apart. And, yes, the eyes of the world would be on them the instant this went public; and yes, cruel comments would be made, but this wasn't about her feelings, but about the island and her promise to Doña Anna to keep it safe. 'How will you explain away the suddenness of our marriage? Coming so soon after the reading of the will, won't it seem odd?'

'I don't have to explain anything,' Xavier assured her.

Of course he didn't. Don Xavier Del Rio didn't play by the rules; he never had. No explanations were necessary.

'I expect the press to report it as a *coup de foudre*, love at first sight, our first meeting having been engineered by my aunt, your employer, Doña Anna. That will get us through for the duration of our marriage.'

'You make our marriage sound more like a prison sentence.' She felt a pang that it couldn't be more, and had to remind herself that a road bridge between fantasy and fact had never existed.

'It will be what you make of it,' Xavier stated. 'It's your idea.'

From the frying pan into the fire, she thought. 'Where will the ball be held?'

'Here, of course.'

Of course. She could forget having a happy, relaxed party amongst friends on the island. The announcement of their impending marriage would be made amongst people she didn't know at a stiff, formal ball.

'Do you have a problem with that?' Xavier probed when she bit down on her lip.

'No. Of course not.'

'In two weeks' time.'

'So soon?' Her heart flipped over. 'Will that be enough time to arrange everything?'

Xavier gave her an amused look. Anything was possible for Don Xavier Del Rio. She'd better get used to it, though a second encounter with high society was not the best start to the plan that she had so boldly put in motion. She could tell he was pleased, because he'd take over now. Their marriage of convenience would be over and done with at breakneck speed.

The night of the ball had arrived. He stared at his stern, formally dressed reflection in the mirror, wondering if Rosie was ready for this. Their last meeting had been here, and when she'd left her face had brightened as if she'd expected him to take her in his arms and seal their bargain with a tender kiss. For her sake, he had resisted any show of affection. It would be wrong to pretend that this wedding was anything more than a convenience for both of them. He admired Rosie for the strength and grace with which she came through the problems she faced, but his cold nature, forged in the bitter past, always triumphed in the end.

He felt nothing for Rosie. So why was he still thinking about her?

His only interest was in seeing how the evening played out, he told himself firmly. Rosie had guts. She would get through it. She had elected to play hardball, and now she had to prove that she could.

Members of so-called high society were already arriving at his gates. The cathedral would be crammed for their wedding. His scandalous match with his late aunt's housekeeper must have kept dinner tables alive with gossip since the invitations went out. Even the ambassador had changed his schedule in order to attend both the wedding and the ball, and the cream of Spanish society would join his guests tonight, together with several members of the royal family. This would not be a low-key affair. Margaret was in charge of arrangements, so he had every confidence that it would all go smoothly. Rosie would not be allowed to put a foot wrong. It remained to be seen what his guests thought of her, but it was what he thought when he saw her after several days apart that intrigued him. His mind was a blank canvas where that was concerned. Would he feel anything more than some fleeting lust when Señorita Clifton arrived at the ball?

* * *

She couldn't have done this without Margaret's help, Rosie reflected, wishing her heart would calm down. It had been thundering for most of the day as she contemplated the evening ahead. Seeing Xavier again was even more daunting than facing his guests at the ball. She'd know at once what he was thinking. She would be able to read his thoughts in his eyes. He might be resigned, or impatient, or... No. Hoping he'd be pleased to see her was too much to ask.

Ball gowns weren't exactly her area of expertise, Rosie fretted as she stared at her reflection in the mirror. 'Do I look all right?'

'You look beautiful,' Margaret assured her as she bustled about, tweaking Rosie's ankle-length gown.

When Margaret had knocked on the door of her suite at the hotel, Rosie had welcomed the friendly older woman with open arms. Finding a ball gown *and* a wedding dress in the time available was way beyond her scope. She had been busily scouring the pages of a magazine, wondering which of the grand boutiques would be likely to let her through the door in her custard dress, when Margaret arrived. She was more a jeans and T-shirt girl, and after the fiasco of the red dress she couldn't risk another disaster. Margaret's down-to-earth encouragement turned out to be just what she'd needed.

Margaret's approval meant a lot to Rosie. She

believed she could trust her to give her an honest opinion. That was what she was waiting for now as Margaret walked a full circle around her.

'I love the gown,' Margaret said as she stared critically at Rosie from every angle. 'It's really stylish, and I've never seen you looking more beautiful.'

'I wouldn't have had a clue what to choose for the ball without you,' Rosie admitted, 'and I certainly wouldn't have known where to shop for it.'

Margaret laughed at this. 'But now you know that when Xavier is involved the designers come to you.'

'And work through the night to get the dresses ready in time,' Rosie added, still marvelling at what was possible for the rich and famous. The designers must have thought it was a love match to rush about as they had. If they'd known the truth, perhaps they wouldn't have been quite so enthusiastic about it, though the scandal alone would make them famous.

'Are you happy, Rosie?' Margaret asked with genuine concern in her voice.

Was she happy? Rosie stared at her face in the mirror, wishing with all her heart that she could confide her fears about the future to Margaret. 'Of course I'm happy,' she said brightly in an attempt to reassure the older woman.

'Then, let's go,' Margaret prompted.

It was too late to change her mind now. Sucking in a deep, steadying breath, she held her head up high as they left the suite together.

* * *

He had expected Margaret and Rosie to arrive long before now. What was keeping them? Surely it was just a matter of picking a dress that fitted and putting it on?

He shifted position impatiently, his stare fixed on the door. All his guests had arrived, and were waiting, as he was, for the most important guest of the night. The evening couldn't have been more perfect. All the doors into the garden had been opened and the sky was littered with stars. The moon was suspended like a silver crescent, resting back on a velvet bed. The orchestra was playing, candles were lit, and chandeliers glittered. Champagne and conversation flowed freely. The ball was already deemed a success. 'And with the additional treat of your special announcement,' one elderly lady had just cooed in his ear. 'None of us can wait for that.'

He could imagine. He disliked being on everyone's tongue and the sooner this was over, the better, as far as he was concerned. The scandal sheets were full of it with incendiary comments about the unsuitability of his marriage. He expected rumbles to go on for quite a while, until some new *cause célèbre* burst upon the public consciousness and everyone forgot about him. He could only hope Margaret had steered Rosie in the right direction. After the unfortunate red dress, a mistake now would attract derision, which would in turn keep the gossip running. Most of his guests were good people, but they did love to talk, and there were piranhas amongst them who loved nothing more than to see a person fall. He could take their scorn, but beneath her bravado Rosie was vulnerable to attack, and, whatever else this match promised, he would not stand by and see her bullied.

He tensed as the room fell silent. Even the musicians had put down their instruments as everyone turned to stare at the door.

Rosie had entered the ballroom.

Standing at the top of the steps, she was framed in light. Her presence coursed through him like a lightning bolt. She was dressed in an exquisite gown of soft, clear blue. The colour was a perfect foil for her glorious red-gold hair. She looked quite astonishingly beautiful. The impact was so staggering it was as if he were seeing her for the very first time. The gown was slim-fitting, and subtly styled with a modest neckline. Beautifully beaded in the same colour as the dress, the fabric sparkled discreetly as she moved. It drew his attention from the loveliness of her face to the perfection of her womanly form. She was the only woman in the room, as far as he was concerned, and his senses soared as she glanced around. Looking for him, he hoped.

Her chin lifted when she saw him and a faint smile touched her lips. The connection between them was immediate, and obvious to everyone else. He didn't care about anyone else, and watched entranced as she walked down the stairs towards him. She'd left her hair loose, the way he liked it, and she was so surprisingly elegant, and yet so painfully vulnerable. He wanted to shield her from all the hungry eyes, but sensed that this walk through the lines of the great and good was something Rosie wanted to do on her own.

Her beauty transfixed every man in the room. His hackles rose as they stared at her. But it was more than Rosie's physical perfection that held him. She was luminous. She had an inner serenity that no other woman could match. She might have been a lost soul from the orphanage when she had first arrived on Isla Del Rey, but Rosie Clifton had found herself tonight, and she was magnificent.

The conductor lifted his baton when she reached the middle of the dance floor, and struck up an elegant Viennese waltz. Some alchemy dictated that Rosie didn't walk towards him, but appeared to float in time to the music as the crowd fell back to let her pass. A collective sigh went up when she reached his side. All thoughts of crude gossip were instantly forgotten. She had silenced the chatterers with nothing more than her poise and innocent appeal.

'Good evening, Xavier.'

'Margaret's done a good job,' he replied dryly, and with maximum understatement.

'I did have some say in it,' she reprimanded him with the hint of a smile.

His groin tightened as she continued to stare levelly into his eyes. 'I'm sure you did,' he agreed, 'and I have to say, you look very beautiful.'

'Do I?' She seemed stunned by his comment.

'Of course you do,' he confirmed, as if this were obvious. 'You're easily the most beautiful woman in the room.'

His senses were in overload. He was in an agony of lust, but something more was happening to him. For all that he boasted of having no feelings, he felt something now, and it was a feeling far more powerful than lust; a feeling that made him want to lead her out of here to somewhere private and quiet. Everything about her: the scent she was wearing, her warmth, her gaze on his face, and her body within inches of his; he could only think she had bewitched him. Remaining cool and detached, as he had intended, was no longer a certainty. His body was like that of a youth with no control.

'I was hoping you'd approve,' she said.

He could see the vulnerability in her eyes. She was so bold, and yet so fragile. Physically, she was small and soft and desirable, and he would have to be made of stone not to want her. 'Do *you* approve?' he murmured. 'I mean, your engagement ball,' he explained, glancing around. He suddenly realised that her answer really mattered to him.

'It's such a beautiful evening. I only hope I don't spoil it for you.'

'I shall have to keep you close all night, to make sure you don't,' he said.

The intimacy between them grew rapidly after that. It was almost as if they were enclosed in a private bubble that excluded all his guests, leaving them on the outside looking in. Rosie laughed and relaxed as he drew her into his arms for the first dance. He would have liked that moment, that very first moment of contact between them, to last for the rest of the night. Her skin felt so warm and soft beneath his touch, and when she closed her hand around his, the desire to protect her overwhelmed him. All thoughts of bargains between them vanished instantly. He was seriously interested in this woman. He wanted her like no other. Judging by the hectic rise and fall of her breasts, she wanted him too. It didn't take long for his thoughts to stray onto the dark side as he contemplated all that innocence aching for his experience to lead the way. It was a feeling that would remain with him for the rest of the night.

His guests applauded politely as he led Rosie in the dance. They were eager to catch their first glimpse of the innocent young housekeeper in the arms of the Spanish Grandee, and had formed a tight circle around them. If they knew Rosie had proposed to him, they wouldn't believe it. That was enough to make him smile. There was the added satisfaction of feeling Rosie tremble when he placed his hand in the small of her back. By the end of the night, his guests would be saying theirs was a love-match. He laughed inwardly at the thought, and almost wished it were true.

CHAPTER TWELVE

MARGARET SMILED ENCOURAGEMENT as Rosie danced with Xavier. If being this close to him hadn't reminded Rosie so vividly of her loss of control at the cocktail party, she might have relaxed, and enjoyed being in his arms. As it was, she felt overwhelmed by what she'd done, and deeply worried for the future of her waning control. Just being this close to him, dancing with him, being in his arms, was enough to cloud her judgement. Being married to him was no guarantee she could handle him. Xavier was so much more experienced than she was. And yet she felt he was right for her in every way. Or was that just this romantic setting and her romantic nature combining? The expression in his eyes was warmer than she'd ever seen it, but—

'Relax,' he said, sensing her tension.

She must relax. She had to hide her feelings. Keeping them under wraps was what had always kept her safe. Xavier was super-intuitive. She had to remember that at all times.

One dance led to another, and then the ambassa-

dor cut in. Xavier yielded to the older man grace-
fully, but when a young royal prince tried to do the
same he wasn't so accommodating. Seeing how tense
he'd become, she politely declined the prince, plead-
ing tiredness as she allowed Xavier to lead her away.

'You have a very beautiful home,' she said as he
escorted her outside. 'You have great taste.'

'My decorators have great taste,' he corrected her.

'The floral displays are exquisite.'

'I'm glad you like them,' he said with a smile that
suggested he'd softened a little.

She thought he'd probably guessed that she was
trying to distract herself from the purpose of the ball.
'Roses are my favourite flowers…'

She wasn't sure he heard her as he led her through
the French doors and onto the veranda overlooking
the exquisite formal gardens. 'I can only imagine
growing up in a place like this.' Resting her fore-
arms on the marble balustrade, she leaned over to
glance around.

'I didn't grow up here.'

She was instantly alert at his tone, which was
tinged with old hurt.

'I went away to school,' he revealed.

'And then you lived with your aunt?'

'In the holidays, yes,' he confirmed in the same
stilted tone.

'You didn't see a lot of your parents.'

She'd struck a nerve, Rosie thought as a muscle
flexed in Xavier's jaw.

'I bought this house with my first fortune,' he said.

'Your first fortune?' she teased, wanting to reach out to him, and not really knowing how.

'I won't deny I've been successful.'

'And why should you? You should be proud of what you've achieved.' Especially after surviving the legacy of bitterness created by his parents' self-indulgent lifestyle, she wanted to add.

'And so should you,' he said, surprising her. 'In some ways, we're not so different, you and I.'

She laughed. 'Just a billion or so apart, and then, of course, there's your title—'

'Which doesn't mean a thing,' he said. 'Come on—' He indicated that she should go ahead of him. 'It's time to go inside so I can make the announcement.'

Her heart banged in her chest at the thought, and she had to remind herself that this was her idea. She knew the moment had to come, but just to hear it said in public would make it real. She had dreamed of this moment since she was a little girl, but had never thought it would be like this. Her dreams had been hazy, involving a handsome lover, and Rosie smiling happily and trustingly into the face of the man she would spend the rest of her life with. Instead, she'd got an arrangement; a marriage of convenience, as Xavier had called it. No one must guess they were faking their emotions, or they would both become figures of ridicule, and her chance to raise support for the island amongst people who mattered would be dust. That didn't stop her wishing the fantasy could come true, and Xavier's announcement would mark the beginning of something wonderful, rather than the beginning of the end.

'Before we go in,' he said, drawing her to one side, 'I want to show you the ring—so there are no surprises,' he explained.

'You've already surprised me,' Rose admitted. 'I didn't expect a ring.'

Xavier frowned as he asked, 'Do you think so little of me?'

'Not at all,' she admitted frankly. 'It's just that I didn't expect anything beyond an announcement of our engagement.'

'Of course there must be a ring,' he said.

'Of course,' she agreed, realising that her comment was further proof of her naivety. The assembled guests would expect her to have an engagement ring. This was Don Xavier Del Rio's fabulously lavish engagement party, after all.

She got another shock, and not a good one, when Xavier flipped the lid on a night-blue velvet box. 'I can't accept that,' she protested, looking at the huge jewel sideways as if it were a snake. To Rosie's eyes, it seemed to be an unnecessarily large stone.

'Why?' he demanded, seeming bemused.

'Because I don't need such a valuable diamond.'

'What did you imagine I would give you?' Xavier demanded, scrutinising the enormous diamond solitaire as if he were seeing it for the first time. 'I can't see anything wrong with this ring.'

'There's nothing wrong with it,' Rosie admitted. 'It's absolutely stunning. It's just not for me.'

Anyone would have been dazzled by the rainbow sparkle thrown off by the magnificent stone. It was a beautiful and obviously priceless gem, but it belonged in a crown, or a sceptre.

And now she had offended him.

'What *do* you want?' he asked, frowning.

'Something smaller and more discreet?'

'Small?' he repeated, as if she had suggested something obscene.

'Small*er*,' she said, knowing they couldn't keep their guests waiting much longer.

'Well, it's too late for that,' he said, 'and, under the circumstances, I think everyone should be left in no doubt that I am fully committed to this match.'

'I'm sorry. You must think me ungrateful.' She only wished there were no barriers between them, and she could really explain how she felt, but she was as much to blame for the distance between them as Xavier. Rosie's childhood had taught her to feel that she wasn't worthy of love, and she guessed that his had taught him pretty much the same. 'I'd rather not wear this,' she said honestly as she handed back the ring. 'Wearing it would feel dishonest to me.'

'Nonsense,' Xavier insisted, but something in his eyes suggested he might just understand. He confirmed her suspicion when he said, 'I do know you a little. That's why I took you aside. I anticipated some reluctance on your part, but we can't disappoint our guests now. We'll go back into the ballroom, where you will smile when I make the formal announcement of our engagement, and gasp with pleasure when I show you the ring.'

It was only the understanding in his eyes that made her agree. 'All right, I'll do it,' she said. Her heart squeezed tight when she saw the relief on his face. 'Of course I'll do it,' she repeated, suddenly filled with the most urgent need to reassure him.

The next day every newspaper carried the story of the fabulous engagement ball at Don Xavier Del Rio's palatial mansion, which had taken yet another eligible bachelor off the scene. Everyone seemed to have been persuaded by their play-acting, Rosie read with relief. She was back at the hotel, and had ordered every newspaper she could think of, so she could check that no one suspected their engagement was a fake, and their subsequent marriage would be a sham. They'd made the headlines, of course, and there were endless shots of Rosie staring lovingly at Xavier, and Xavier smiling down at his fiancée. There were even more shots of the ring, and from every possible angle. *'The ring of the century'* some were saying, as if the fabulous jewel were a weather condition that had blown everyone away.

As far as Rosie was concerned the ring was a monstrous billboard, reminding her of her mistake in ever thinking this plan made sense. How could she play-act a marriage to Xavier, when she was fast developing feelings for him? And to make matters worse, they were feelings that would only be dismissed and discarded by Xavier, who wasn't capable of feeling anything.

The ring was also a huge responsibility, Rosie reflected, tossing the newspaper aside, and one she had no interest in keeping. The diamond was so big and heavy it kept swinging around her finger, and she didn't dare to take it off in case she lost it. She knew she was being ungrateful, but the ring seemed to represent everything that was wrong with their match. She held the ring up to the light. It was so big it looked unreal. So, perhaps it was the perfect ring, after all...

She was going to keep her promise to Doña Anna but at a far higher price than she'd imagined. If she and Xavier were lucky enough to have a child, she would love that baby with every fibre of her being, and defend it fiercely from hurt, but would Xavier do the same, or was the idea of an heir just a figure of speech to him?

One of the worst parts of the ball had been speaking to the islanders after the announcement of their engagement. Xavier had invited a group of them to the ball. Trying to join in their excitement at the news of their engagement had torn her in two. She hated the pretence, and wondered if Xavier had noticed that she'd left the ball almost immediately after talking to them. Seeing she was upset, Margaret had stepped in, calling for the driver to take Rosie back to the hotel. Rosie had slipped away while Xavier had been talking to the ambassador. She hadn't wanted to interrupt him, or give him the chance to try to stop her leaving. She'd played her part. She had been charming to all his guests, and they'd been charming back, now that she was to marry such a prominent member of the aristocracy. Safely back at the hotel, she'd stared at herself in the mirror, hardly recognising the woman in the exquisite dress. She'd washed her face, put on her cotton PJ's, and had fallen into bed exhausted, sleeping fitfully as she dreamed about an impossibly handsome man, dancing the night away with an impossibly naïve woman, who didn't have a clue what tomorrow held.

She sprang alert at the sound of a knock on the door. Breakfast. Thank goodness! She was starving. She'd been too nervous to eat before the ball, and during it she had been with—

'Xavier?'

She stood back from the door as he strode in. 'Are you all right? If I'd known you were coming…' Smoothing her hair, she tightened the belt on the hotel's towelling robe. He looked as if he hadn't slept for a week. His stubble was thick. His hair was tangled. He had obviously tugged on the first jeans he'd found.

'Everyone wondered where you got to last night,' he said, swinging around to face her.

Was he angry, or was he concerned about her? She couldn't tell. His eyes were ravaged with exhaustion, and his body looked unbearably tense.

'I stayed at the ball until almost midnight.'

'I know when you left,' he said. 'And you left without a word to your host.' He angled his chin, his black eyes firing questions at her.

'My fiancé,' she corrected him in a timely reminder that they had both made a pledge last night in front of hundreds of witnesses.

'You should have stayed. We have a lot to talk through.'

'Like…?' she prompted, unconsciously twisting the belt on her robe until it started to cut into her hand.

Like how he felt about fathering a child, Xavier thought, when there was no possibility of him developing a talent for empathy, or learning parenting skills in the time available. 'Like your views on becoming a mother,' he said. 'Are you ready for it? You're very young.'

'But I feel as if I've been preparing for this all my life. Surely you must know how I feel? I've dreamed of nothing but having a family of my own for as long as I can remember.'

'But not forming that family like this, surely?'

'If your heir means nothing more to you than securing the island, then, yes, I do have doubts,' she admitted.

'For the child,' he said, nodding agreement. 'So

you can only hope I'll feel differently once the child is born?'

'Maybe you never will,' she said, her eyes searching his. 'Or, maybe you're worried that you won't be able to feel any different when you're a father.'

'I'm supposed to experiment on a child? I'm supposed to wait to see how I feel when it's born?' he exclaimed, growing increasingly heated.

'I hope you know that's not what I meant,' Rosie said with real concern. She'd never seen him like this before. 'Both of us knew this would never be easy.'

'Easy?' He huffed an ugly laugh. 'That's an understatement. Are you saying you want to pull out?'

He sounded almost hopeful. 'You should know me better than that,' she said firmly.

'Maybe you want me to slow down—give you more time?' Xavier suggested.

'What difference would waiting make?'

He seemed to be the one needing reassurance, and so she admitted quietly, 'My only concern is for the baby.' She couldn't help but smile. Her heart was full to overflowing at the thought of a child. 'A child needs security and a proper home—'

Xavier cut her off with an impatient gesture. 'A Del Rio child will have everything it needs. And the ring?' he prompted, moving on from one subject to the next as if they held equal importance. He looked for it on her hand.

'Here—' The diamond had swung around again. She righted it, and put out her hand so he could see

it. 'Take it and put it away somewhere safe. Return
it to the jeweller, if you can. It's served its purpose.'
She tried to pull the ring off her finger, but the band
was so tight she couldn't get it over her knuckle.

'Leave it where it is,' he said. 'There's no going
back. You made a promise.'

'And I will keep that promise, with or without
this ring.'

Leaving him, she went to the bathroom to find
some shampoo to ease the ring off her finger.

'Here,' she said, going back into the room and
holding it out to him.

'You're sure about this?' he said, hesitating before taking it back.

'I'm absolutely certain.' What purpose would a
flashy ring serve on the island? She wouldn't wear
anything that might put distance between her and
the people she cared about.

As he took the ring their hands touched, and she
felt the same heat and the same longing she always
felt when he was close. Her gaze flew to his, and, of
course, he was watching her. His grip on her hand
slowly moved to her wrist, and from there to her
sensitive upper arm, until he was bringing her close
and dipping his head and kissing her, and she was
clinging to him, with need and want, and tears were
stinging the backs of her eyes.

This was insane. She was asking to be hurt.

'I haven't slept all night, thanks to you,' he growled.

'You must have a guilty conscience,' she said,

burying her growing feelings for him beneath another joke. 'I slept like a baby.'

'Liar,' he murmured against her kiss-bruised mouth. He caged her against the wall with one hand planted above her head and his other caressing her cheek. 'I know this isn't easy for you—'

'But it's the best—the only solution,' she insisted, trying to convince herself. She'd come up with the solution out of sheer desperation, and now it was up to her to shut her mind to the hurt waiting in the wings.

'I've never made allowances for another person's feelings before,' Xavier admitted, his dark stare blazing into hers. 'Maybe I'm clumsy at it.'

'You're terrible at it,' she assured him, curving a smile. 'But that's only because you've never allowed yourself to care for anyone.'

'Are you calling me a coward?' he challenged softly.

'Where feelings are concerned? Yes. I am.'

'You have the same problem,' he argued. 'You've never risked your heart.'

'Which is why I understand you.' She met the challenge in his eyes with a level stare.

'Do you understand me?' Xavier queried. He looped his arms around her waist and stared down at her. 'If you do, you must know that the ring was a showstopper, designed for that purpose. I asked for something striking and I got it.'

'You didn't go to a store, then?'

He frowned. 'I commissioned it from the royal jewellers, of course.'

'Of course you did.' She began to laugh.

'What's so funny?' he queried, but warmth was beginning to glow in his eyes.

'You,' she said. 'You're funny.'

He stared at her for a moment, and then brushed a gentle kiss across her lips. He always made her heart ache for so much more and that was dangerous. Understanding what made someone tick was the first step to growing close.

'I always knew billionaires didn't shop on the High Street like everyone else,' she said, trying to avoid the risk to her heart with some humour.

CHAPTER THIRTEEN

'I'M SORRY YOU don't like the ring, but, as ours was never supposed to be a genuine engagement, I thought it didn't matter.'

He was right, but each of his words was like a stab to her heart. 'Even if ours had been a real engagement, I don't need jewellery like that,' she said. 'I'd have no use for it,' she added with a shrug. 'I'm just as happy threading daisies for a crown.'

'You can't make a ring out of daisies,' Xavier pointed out.

'A piece of string, then.' She laughed. 'But, please, no more diamonds the size of duck eggs. Okay?'

'The ring was just a prop for the drama we're engaged in,' Xavier said, shrugging it off. 'It had to make an impact, and look convincing in print, and I think it did that.'

'My piece of string would have caused more of a stir,' Rosie argued, slanting one of her grins at him.

'And been far more you,' Xavier agreed, his dark eyes dancing with laughter. 'But that wasn't what last night was about,' he said, turning serious. 'It was about convincing everyone that this is real, so you get the credibility you want, and I get the one thing money can't buy.'

A child. Xavier's heir.

'But now I'm afraid I've got some bad news for you.'

Her heart lurched with dread.

'I'm going away on business for a few days.'

'Is that all?' Her relief was obvious. 'That's good news for me, surely?' she teased, determined to keep things light between them. 'So, what have you come here for? To get the ring and make sure I don't bolt while you're away?' She could see she had hit the mark from the expression in his eyes. 'Don't worry. I'll be here when you get back, and I'll be at your side for the wedding. We will be married, and we will see this through.'

'And I promise you won't have anything to worry about.'

She wanted to laugh hysterically at that comment.

'Everything's in hand,' Xavier assured her. 'Our wedding will be held in the cathedral, with a reception at my mansion afterwards. Transport has been organised, so all you have to do is put on the dress and turn up.'

'Right.' She nodded her head as if she were accepting directions to a café in town, and had to remind herself that theirs was a marriage of convenience, and that that was how such things played out. Theirs was not a meeting of two hearts.

She might have thought up this idea, but she couldn't help wishing their wedding day could be something more than this meticulously planned arrangement.

'It will be a grand affair,' Xavier told her without apology.

Fabulously lavish, she translated.

'I hope you're all right with that?'

And if she wasn't?

'I'm fine with that,' she lied.

'No expense will be spared. I'll make it a day for you to remember.'

Was that a promise or a threat? She had no doubt their wedding would be a spectacularly extravagant day. Without intimacy. Without meaning. Without love.

'You will stay on at the hotel,' Xavier went on, as if she had any choice. 'The designer will return for a last fitting of the dress, while make-up artists and hairdressers will attend you on the day. It will be easier for you to stay here than to go back to the island. Don't look so worried. I guarantee I'll be back for the wedding.'

'It would be a half-hearted affair without you,' she joked weakly.

'Does nothing get you down, Rosie Clifton?'

Plenty. The lack of love in their arrangement got her down. She had never expected any, and so she couldn't admit to being disappointed in that direction. Her concern for a child not yet born got her down even more. She had done what she had thought was for the best, and was now left with the growing suspicion that she'd only made things worse. Was this what Doña Anna had intended?

'If anything gets me down, I'll bounce back up again,' she said in an attempt to convince herself as much as Xavier. Exactly how she was going to do that, she didn't have a clue.

'This is a difficult situation for both of us,' Xavier remarked. 'Doña Anna was always tricky to handle, but her swan song takes some beating. And you definitely don't want the ring? You can keep it if you want to,' he offered.

'I definitely don't want it,' Rosie confirmed with a wry smile. 'Honestly, it's absolutely unnecessary.'

Something like admiration crossed Xavier's face, and then he stowed the ring away in the back pocket of his jeans as if it were a penny sweet. 'What are you thinking about now?' he prompted with interest when she frowned and chewed her lip.

'I was thinking back to the orphanage,' she admitted.

'Look forward instead,' Xavier advised.

Rosie had been remembering when she used to sit on a scraggy patch of grass with her chin on her knees, dreaming about her wedding day. The day would be all misty white, and she would be dressed in a billowing gown. There would be crowds of guests and loads of flowers, and a fabulously handsome husband would be waiting to take her away from the colourless institution.

'I was just dreaming about happily-ever-after,' she admitted recklessly. 'I know it won't come to that for us, because ours is an arrangement, but maybe it won't be all bad?'

'I hope not,' he said with feeling. 'And dreams are free, Rosie Clifton, so you can dream all you like.'

In less than a week her dream would be dust.

'Your life has changed now,' Xavier told her, 'so no more talk of the orphanage.'

She still felt as if she were on the outside looking in.

'Rosie?' Xavier prompted, seeing her abstraction. 'I think we should lay this ghost once and for all,' he said in a voice she couldn't ignore. 'I want you to tell me about your worst time in the orphanage.'

'Do you really want to know?'

'I really do,' he said.

She wouldn't tell him about her wedding day fantasy. He'd think her soft. 'Christmas was the worst time,' she said after a moment's thought.

'Why?' He frowned.

'Because well-intentioned people arrived with gifts, and that gave us children a tantalising glimpse of the outside world.'

'But surely you'd rather have those people come to visit at Christmas than not?'

'Of course, and I don't mean to sound ungrateful.' But she had felt like an animal in the zoo, to be cooed over, petted and fed a titbit before the visitors went away again. She had always imagined the visitors returning to their warm and cosy homes to open their presents beneath a massive Christmas tree, before stuffing themselves with food until they couldn't stand up. But what had given her the biggest pang of all was the thought of them sharing the happiness of a family united over the holiday season. How she'd envied that, until she'd found the same warmth and welcome waiting for her on the island. 'I'm frightened our wedding's going to be like that,' she admitted.

'Like what?' Xavier pulled back his head with surprise. 'What's wrong with Christmas?'

'Absolutely nothing. I'm just afraid that I'll be put on show at our wedding, and then whisked away to be impregnated with the Del Rio heir.'

'For goodness' sake,' Xavier exclaimed. 'What a thing to say. And now you're shivering.' He drew her close. 'I didn't realise you were so upset about it. Why didn't you say?'

'I'm dreading it,' she admitted.

'The impregnation, or the wedding?'

His delivery was so deadpan she couldn't help but laugh.

'That's better,' Xavier said softly.

Rosie's laugh sounded brittle to him. It made him want to take her in his arms and reassure her, and only his desire to keep her safe from him was stopping him. 'What has my aunt done?' he murmured, speaking his thoughts out loud.

'Brought us together to torment us, I think,' Rosie observed in her usual down-to-earth way. 'And for better or for worse, this time.'

'My thoughts exactly,' he agreed. Bringing her into his arms, he gave her a hug. What harm could one hug do? 'Whatever this is or isn't between us,' he said, pulling his head back to stare at her, 'I promise I'll make it easy for you. You don't have anything to be frightened of—in bed, or out of it. And as for the rest, you'll have Margaret's support all the way. Better?' he murmured when she seemed to relax.

Worse. Far, far worse. She wanted the fantasy she'd dreamed of so much it hurt. She didn't need Xavier's money, or his name, but she did need this warm, caring man, the man who lay deep beneath the armour Xavier had built so successfully around his heart.

Seducing Rosie would be all too easy. She had a touching eagerness to experience everything life had to offer. She had shocked him disappearing at midnight without warning, but her unpredictability was one of the qualities he liked best about her. Yes, it annoyed the hell out of him, but doormats bored him, and gold-diggers were ten a penny. He doubted anyone could cage this wild bird. The thought that anyone might try to do so enraged him. No one would take away Rosie Clifton's freedom, if he had anything to say about it, not even him.

'You look grim,' she said, pulling back to stare at him.

'Do I?' He shrugged. He should be smiling at the thought that Rosie had proved he had some small shred of humanity left. She had made him care what happened to her, when he'd thought he was incapable of feeling, and she'd made him care for the island all over again.

'I hope you're not looking grim because you're thinking about our wedding,' she said.

He had been thinking about their wedding, but not in the way Rosie imagined. They would marry, and he hoped an heir would follow, but instead of him breaking it off then, he would set her free as she deserved, and with her bright face right in front of him he was suddenly dreading the thought of doing that. 'I've got a plane to catch,' he said, reluctantly easing away from her. 'So I'll see you at the altar—'

'With a modest ring, I hope,' she teased.

They shared a smile. His was cynical, hers was guileless. 'I'll see what I can do,' he promised.

'Safe journey,' she called out as he made for the door.

He turned around. She was still smiling, still employing the eternal optimism that had kept her upbeat throughout her years in the orphanage. He hoped it would continue to help her now.

* * *

Rosie's wedding day dawned as every bride hoped it would, with sunshine and birdsong outside the window.

But every bride hoped for company to share her happy day, and she didn't expect to face the start of that day alone in her hotel room.

She'd always been alone, and she'd always got through, Rosie reassured herself. Margaret had been with her for most of the week and Margaret couldn't be expected to be around 24/7. She would have her own preparations to make. Margaret was a guest of honour at the ceremony; the ceremony the press was calling the wedding of the year.

This wasn't a marriage in the real sense, Rosie told herself firmly as she jumped out of bed, so she had nothing to worry about.

Their wedding night would be real enough.

Yes, well, she'd handle that too. She didn't have time to think about it now. She had other things to do—a shower to take, and her courage to buckle on, along with the blue garter the designer had insisted she must wear high up on her thigh under her dress... where only Rosie's husband would see it.

What did the woman imagine? That theirs was a love match?

Why wouldn't she, when the whole world thought that was exactly what it was?

Pausing on her way to take a shower, she trailed her fingertips reverently across the exquisite Swiss lace skirt of her gown. Her wedding dress was everything a fantasy wedding dress should be. An entire workroom had spent the limited time available working through the night to make sure it was ready in time, and Rosie couldn't have loved it more. She had promised herself that at least for the few short hours of the ceremony, she would believe in the dream. It wouldn't hurt anyone if she did so.

Her heart began to flutter as she thought about Xavier, and what he would be doing now. She was missing him. She hadn't seen him since he went away, and, however much of a charade this was, she was certain they were drawing closer. If she teased him he took it well, instead of standing on his dignity. She only wished they could both unwind the past and start over, with no hang-ups standing in their way, but she suspected no one entered a marriage completely clean in that sense.

She turned at a knock on the door. Breakfast. She raced to open the door to her suite, not wanting to keep the server waiting.

'Margaret!' She'd never been more relieved to see anyone in her life.

'I thought I should pop in.' Margaret darted a quick glance around the room. 'I'm not intruding, am I?'

'Not at all—I'm alone. Please come in! It's good of you to spare the time when I know you must be busy.'

'Nonsense,' Margaret declared. 'Who's busier than the bride? All I need to do is to put on a dab of lipstick and a suit that isn't tweed, and I'm done. I was wondering if you'd got something old to wear,' Margaret continued on as she shrugged off her sensible mac and cast it aside on a chair. 'You know the old saying, Something old, something new, something borrowed, something blue— Ah, I see you have that.' Margaret's shrewd eyes twinkled as she surveyed the dress and the garter hanging around the neck of the padded hanger. 'The dress is new, the garter is blue, and I've brought my tiny beaded reticule for you to *borrow* for the reception, and I've brought something that belonged to my mother for you—a small gift from me to wish you well. They can be your something old,' she said.

'I can't possibly accept a gift like this,' Rosie breathed as Margaret showed her the small pearl stud earrings. They were the perfect finishing touch for the dress, but she was overwhelmed by the gift, by the thought, and by the kindness behind it.

'Of course you can accept them,' Margaret insisted with a warm smile as she closed Rosie's hand around her present. 'Now, come on,' she chivvied. 'We don't want to be anything more than fashionably late. We'll have breakfast together, and then I'll help you to dress.'

The moment Rosie saw the cathedral with its tall spires and intricate carvings she made a promise to make her vows sincerely. Whatever her situation, she would show respect for the church, and for everyone who had entered the same portals with their hearts full of emotion. As she stepped out of the limousine she reminded herself that she'd always been resilient. She would go through with this, and she would make it work. Margaret was waiting to organise the billowing silk chiffon train, with its liberal scattering of diamanté and seed pearls. The dress was so beautiful that the assembled onlookers gasped when they caught their first sight of it.

Lifting her chin, Rosie mounted the steps slowly and alone. She had explained to Margaret that she wanted to do this, as this was her journey, and her decision, and she was determined that she wouldn't fail in any part of it. Margaret didn't know the whole story; she'd never asked, but she respected Rosie's decision. Having given the organist the prearranged signal when the bride arrived, Margaret followed Rosie into the church.

As the crashing chords of the organ rang out, the voices of the choir soared in a triumphal anthem. *Was all this for her?* For a split second, Rosie couldn't move. Her feet simply refused to obey her brain's instructions, and her throat was so very tight, she doubted she'd be able to say her vows. The cathedral was packed. There didn't seem to be a single free seat. The scent of incense was so heavy she could hardly breathe. She looked for Xavier, but it was like looking down the wrong end of a telescope, and she had a legion of curious guests to walk through before she could reach his side. Then he turned and his dark stare blazed into hers. An unbreakable bond seemed to connect them, drawing her towards him, and now she noticed the roses: Arctic roses, the same roses that grew so bravely in the garden at the hacienda.

She took the flowers as a signal. Even if they were just coincidence, rather than a loving gesture from Xavier, his promise to make this a happy and special day looked as if it might come true.

The roses kept her on track. She thought of them as emergency lights in the cabin of a jet, leading her towards him, and almost laughed at the thought. She quickly governed her face in front of the dignitaries present. She didn't want them thinking she was nervous, or over-faced by the occasion. It was a relief to reach Xavier's side. He looked stunning, every bit the Spanish Grandee. She responded to him with yearning as she came to a halt at his side. She sucked in a shaking breath as he lifted her veil, and was surprised by the warmth in his eyes. He was thanking her, she told herself sensibly. He was probably relieved she'd turned up.

'And now you may kiss the bride...'

Is it really over?

Up to that point, everything had been dreamy and virginal, white, but now the world shot into vivid colour. Xavier's blood-red sash of office, which he wore over his dark, formal suit, made Rosie remember their wedding night. The voices of the choir soared even higher in celebration as Xavier dipped his head to chastely kiss her on both cheeks. She closed her eyes, but all she could think about was what lay ahead of her when they were finally alone. But she smiled when she looked at the wedding ring on her finger.

'Do you like it?' Xavier asked.

'I love it,' she said honestly. 'It's the perfect ring for me.' It was a plain band, with no stones or ornamentation. If they'd been a proper couple and had gone shopping for rings together, she couldn't have found anything to please her more.

'It's time, Rosie,' Xavier prompted.

She turned with him to face the congregation, and, linking her arm through his, she allowed Xavier to lead her forward to greet the world as his wife.

CHAPTER FOURTEEN

THE RECEPTION SEEMED ENDLESS. Rosie ate little and tried not to think too much, while the hours passed in a haze of good wishes and congratulations. She was only just coming to terms with the yawning gap between an idea and an accomplished fact. Her throat tightened as she gazed at Xavier. His expression was governed for the public and it was impossible to read his thoughts. An encouraging smile from Margaret put her back on track. She was no longer the bemused orphan, revelling in the simple pleasures of freedom on a beautiful island, but a wife and property owner, with huge responsibilities. She had married a Spanish Grandee, who had centuries of tradition behind him, but as well as all her duties she had to be true to herself.

When the Master of Ceremonies indicated that the guests must be silent and Xavier rose to his feet to speak she knew the end of the celebration was in sight. Xavier was as commanding as ever, and she was pleased that he remembered to acknowledge his debt to Doña Anna.

'For bringing me a wife,' he said, turning to look at Rosie. That look sent sparks flying through her. 'And now you must excuse us,' he added when the applause had died down. 'My bride and I are leaving.'

Her stomach flipped when he turned to look at her again. She only wished she could thrill as she had the first time, but now she was facing the thought of being alone with him, and that meant confronting the greatest demon of all: her fear that sex brought pain, and disaster followed. That was the legend in the orphanage, and she'd seen nothing since then to change her mind.

'We have an appointment with the tide,' Xavier explained genially to their guests. He reached out a hand to help her from her chair. 'And the tide waits for no man,' he added in an intimate murmur, staring deep into her eyes.

'Not even you?' she challenged, demanding a last burst of energy from the spirit that had kept her going throughout the day.

'Not even me,' he confirmed in the same low, husky whisper. 'Please stay for as long as you like,' he added to their guests. 'There will be fireworks at midnight.'

Maybe even before that, Rosie thought dryly, recognising impending hysteria when it came knocking.

Xavier took hold of her hand in a firm grip, flashing awareness through her veins as he led her from the table.

'What about my things?' she said, pulling back. Everything she owned was still at the hotel.

'You can have your things sent on,' he told her. 'And you'll have new things where we're going.'

He'd waited long enough, she guessed, and no more stops would be made along the way.

A helicopter was waiting for them on the lawn outside. Xavier was the pilot.

'Where are we going?' she asked through the mic attached to her headphones when she was safely strapped into the passenger seat beside him.

'It's a surprise.'

Xavier's voice sounded metallic and distant in her ears as they lifted off. They flew over the twinkling lights of the city and headed out to sea. Now there was only blackness surrounding them, and overhead the moon, until she saw the great white ship, looming out of the darkness, impossibly large and impossibly sleek. She'd heard about super-yachts, but had never seen one before.

'Is it yours?' Of course it was his, she thought as Xavier started talking through his mic in preparation for landing. Don Xavier Del Rio's wealth was incalculable, and this was just one more symbol of his power.

As the helicopter sank lower she recognised the sleek black launch on which Xavier had first arrived on Isla Del Rey. It was just one toy amongst many on board this billionaire's ocean-going yacht. 'How big is it?' she asked when he'd ended his call.

'The length of twelve of your London double-decker buses,' he said, settling the helicopter smoothly on its skids.

'Not that big, then,' she teased, hoping to reclaim some of the warmth they'd shared at their wedding reception. For some reason, Xavier seemed all business now—distant and preoccupied.

Switching off the engine, he removed her headphones. When his fingertips brushed her face she wanted him to kiss her, and like a fool closed her eyes. When nothing happened she opened them again to find he'd moved away.

'Wait there,' he said. 'I'll lift you down so you don't trip over your dress. Welcome to my world,' he added dryly.

Would she ever be ready for his world? Rosie wondered as Xavier opened her door and the clean fresh scent of ozone replaced the warm air inside the cabin. She couldn't imagine a time when she would ever get used to this billionaire lifestyle, and had to hide her apprehension when he helped her out, before escorting her down a seemingly endless line of crew waiting to welcome them.

Everyone seemed so happy to see her, and that almost made it worse. She hated deceiving the crew—like the islanders before them—and almost wished their marriage could be what it seemed.

Xavier insisted on carrying her over the threshold into their suite of rooms. The moment he closed the door and set her down in the middle of a huge and very opulent bedroom, she felt small and insignificant, and smothered by huge wealth and privilege.

What on earth had possessed her to think this would work? Rosie agonised for the umpteenth time. She'd have plenty of opportunity to find out. They were quite alone. No one would disturb them here. She was fast discovering how many layers of insulation lay between the super-rich and the rest of the world.

She still grouped herself very firmly with *the rest*, Rosie determined as Xavier loosened the neck of his shirt. Shrugging off his jacket, he tossed it on a chair.

He looked at her properly for the first time since the reception. 'You'd better turn around so I can help you out of that dress.'

Her mouth dried. She'd known this was coming, but still…

She turned and tried to concentrate on the thick rugs beneath her feet, and how beautifully they were woven in the most amazing multitude of jewel colours, but, however hard she tried to distract herself from what was happening, her gaze kept flashing to the crisp white linen sheets on the huge, teak-framed bed. Xavier had brought her straight into the bedroom. No time to lose when it came to making an heir—

'Forgive me,' he said, maybe sensing something of her apprehension. 'Would you like a drink first?'

She swallowed deep. 'Water, please.'

She seized the chance to take in her surroundings when he went to pour a glass from the crystal jug placed ready for him beside the bed. Polished wood and burnished brass provided a suitably classy setting for artefacts from all over the world. Crystal lights illuminated exquisite works of art, paintings that told stories as eloquent as the books they both loved. She glanced at Xavier's back, and thought again how attractive he was. If only there had been more time to get to know him better. Maybe it was all business for him now they were married, and they wouldn't have a proper conversation again. *Outside bed.*

There were several low brass tables, laden with food and drink, suggesting he planned to remain in the bedroom for quite some time. Her pulse went crazy at the thought, while her mouth turned drier than ever.

'Your water,' he said, handing her the glass.

'Thank you.'

She took a great gulp, and when he moved behind her she almost took a bite out of the glass rim. When his warm hands touched her naked back, her body quivered with awareness. The sound of the laces on her gown sliding through silk and snapping free made her start to shiver all over again. She wasn't wearing a bra, as support was built into the dress.

Xavier brushed the gown from her shoulders in one smooth move. It pooled on the rug at her feet. He removed her veil and smoothed her hair. Brushing her hair aside, he kissed the nape of her neck until she shivered with arousal, and then he encouraged her to turn around, so she was standing in front of him naked.

'No stockings?' he murmured, his mouth tugging with the humour she had so desperately hoped would return.

'No shoes, either,' she confessed.

'How long have you been barefoot?' He frowned, pretending to be stern.

'Since you met me?' She slanted a rueful smile.

'You were wearing flip-flops when I first met you.' His husky voice was warm with humour. 'So now you're my wife, you're determined to go barefoot?'

'Only because my wedding shoes pinched.'

He laughed, a rumble low in his chest. 'Of course, you took your shoes off,' he said with an accepting shrug. 'You're Rosie.'

'I was a bride with sore feet,' she argued softly, wondering if she dared hope that Xavier was trying to put her at her ease. She wasn't embarrassed standing in front of him naked. She was like an open book, waiting to see what would fill the next chapter. Something about her manner must have touched him, because he took her face very gently in his hands to kiss her as she'd always dreamed her husband would

kiss her on her wedding night. It was a gentle and un-
demanding kiss, and when she responded, softening
and sighing, he pushed his fingers through her hair
to cradle her scalp, holding her with extreme tender-
ness, as if she were very precious to him. This was
not the fiery passion that had consumed them once
before, but the start of a very thorough seduction, she
suspected. Xavier could make love to her with nothing more than teasing kisses that made her want so
much more. His lips were warm and persuasive, and
when his tongue demanded possession of her mouth,
she couldn't refuse him anything.

Lifting her into his arms, he carried her to the bed.
Laying her down, he stood back and undressed. He
was like a statue cast in bronze, deeply tanned, and
brutally beautiful. She stared at him in awe.

'Touch me,' he said, joining her on the bed.

When she hesitated he took hold of her hands and
guided her fingers across his muscular chest, and on
over the ridged muscles of his belly. 'Hold me,' he
commanded softly.

Her anxious gaze flew to his face and she shook
her head.

'Why not?' he whispered, his stare dark and long.

'Because I've never done anything like this before, and I'll probably get it horribly wrong.'

He smiled. 'What's to get wrong?' Drawing her
into his arms, he guided her, and when she gasped,
he asked, 'Did I scorch you?'

Only her heart.

'Do I frighten you, Rosie?'

Lifting her head, she stared steadily into his eyes. 'No. You don't frighten me, Xavier.'

He kissed her, and within moments he deepened the kiss. He could soothe and arouse her all at the same time, and explore her body until she was whimpering with need. Lacing her fingers through his hair, she closed her eyes and basked in pleasure.

Nudging one hard-muscled thigh between her legs, he worked some magic with his hands that made her forget her fears. Arching her body towards him, she searched for more contact, more pleasure, and when he cupped her buttocks in his big, strong hands to hold her in place as he pleasured her, cries of need poured from her throat. She needed this— needed him.

'Not enough?' he murmured.

'No,' she exclaimed.

'And now?' he whispered.

She was beyond speech by this time, and could only exhale raggedly and shake her head.

'Enough?' he said as he caught just the tip of his erection inside her.

'No—' The word was torn from her throat.

Pinning her wrists above her head, he brought his face close to ask, 'Do you trust me?'

'Yes… I trust you.'

And so he stroked and dipped and pulled away again, until she was writhing beneath him, helpless with frustration. She needed so much more than he seemed prepared to give her. But then, very slowly, and all the time holding her gaze, he sank deep.

There was a moment, the very briefest of moments, when her body yielded to him and she felt a pinprick of discomfort. It was enough for her to briefly forget the erotic trance into which he'd placed her, but he had expected this, and now he soothed her with tender words and gentle kisses, until all she could think about was him.

Xavier took her slowly and carefully until he was lodged deep inside her, where he rested for a moment, giving her a chance to become used to the sensation. And then he worked his hips until she was clinging to the edge of the precipice with her fingertips. One deep, firm thrust, and she fell, gratefully claiming her release with shocked and greedy cries of pleasure, and when she finally quietened there was only one word on her lips, and that was, 'More.'

Xavier withdrew almost completely before taking her again, and this time he wasn't so gentle, or so considerate and slow. And she loved it even more than the first time.

'More?' he suggested, his mouth tugging in a wicked smile as she groaned rhythmically in time with the subsiding waves of pleasure. He didn't wait for her answer, and plunged deep. She was more than ready for him when he commanded. 'Now!'

'Let me ride you,' she insisted when she was calm enough to speak. 'I want to do more than lie here and be pleasured.'

'You'll find no argument from me,' he agreed. Lifting her into position, he said, 'Take me.'

She needed no encouragement, especially when Xavier thrust his hips towards her to a dependable beat, applying pressure exactly where she needed it.

Throwing her head back, she allowed him to hold her and guide her. She loved the way he liked to watch. She wanted to make it last for as long as she could, but Xavier made that impossible. Taking a firm hold of her hips, he upped both pressure and speed until her mounting cries of excitement became wails of release.

And that release was so fierce for both of them she didn't have the strength to do more than collapse exhausted onto his chest when it was done. And even then the pleasure continued to pulse through her, until finally she drew a deep, contented breath and fell asleep.

CHAPTER FIFTEEN

SHE WOKE TO find Xavier making love to her. He was behind her, moving slowly, but steadily, rhythmically, lazily thrusting, so that her pleasure level on waking was exquisitely extreme. Leaning forward, she raised her hips, making herself even more available for him. She knew he liked to watch. Every action has a reaction, she thought, smiling to herself as he groaned with pleasure and upped the pace. He couldn't wait and neither could she, and very soon both of them were driven by a fierce hunger that could only have one ending.

'You're insatiable,' he murmured with approval when her cries of pleasure had finally died down.

'And you are very good at what you do,' Rosie admitted, groaning with satisfaction as she rested back.

Xavier raised himself on one elbow to stare down at her. Dawn was peeping through the drapes, illuminating his face. He looked more disreputable than ever. Morning was kind to him. His wild hair was dishevelled, while his stubble was thicker, sharper, blacker, and, best of all, he was smiling lazily at her with that rare smile that meant so much to her. She leaned forward to plant a kiss on his lips.

Xavier's answer to that was to turn her beneath him. He had no need to prepare her. She was ready and groaned with contentment when he sank deep. He made no pretence of drawing things out this time, and they moved urgently towards the longed-for goal. When his warmth flooded her, she felt a great, almost primal sense of completion. She had never been so happy in all her life. Resting back on the pillows, she turned her wedding ring round and round, making it glitter in the growing light.

'I think you like that ring,' Xavier commented huskily.

'I love it,' Rosie admitted. The simple gold band seemed to represent everything that was right about them. The circle was complete—almost. It would be complete when they went back to the island and started to work there together.

She turned with surprise as Xavier swung off the bed. Reaching out, she tried to catch hold of him, but he eluded her. 'I have to work,' he said. 'Nothing's changed where that's concerned.'

'What happened to the time you could always take off?' she argued.

'I can't take time off today,' he said, seeming preoccupied. 'There's plenty for you to do on board,' he added, as if she were a child in need of entertainment.

Was that it? He'd made efforts to impregnate her, not once, but many times. Did he consider the job done now? A wave of cold dread washed over her. She couldn't pretend she wasn't bewildered as she watched him stroll naked across the room, and she wasn't sure how to respond.

'Take a shower and then a swim, if you like,' he added. 'There are two pools, a cinema, and a gym—or a reading room, if you prefer. I'll see you later—'

'Later?' She sat bolt upright in the bed. 'When, later? Will I see you at lunch?'

'I thought the idea was that we make no demands on each other,' Xavier commented as he closed the door on his dressing room.

True. But that didn't make it any easier to accept.

It was only later when she came out of the shower and heard the helicopter taking off, she realised that Xavier wasn't just leaving her to go to his study, or to some other room on the vessel, he was actually taking a trip. She had no idea how long he'd be gone. He hadn't given her an agenda. And this was supposed to be their honeymoon—

Get over it, Rosie told herself impatiently as she towelled down after her shower. She hadn't married a pipe-and-slippers man, and this wasn't one of her fantasies that she could tailor to suit herself. She had to accept every facet of Xavier's complicated life. But that didn't mean she had to sit around on her backside, waiting to see what he might do next.

She had a super-yacht to explore, and plans of her own to make, now that she had the means to do so.

But this time the instruction from her can-do spirit had a very hollow ring to it.

Gathering up her wedding dress from the floor, she spread it out carefully on the sofa. Her gaze lingered on the beautiful workmanship. Hours of work had gone into the exquisite dress. *And for what?*

Stop that! She might be naïve in some things, but she had never been pathetic. She had to get used to the idea of being Xavier's convenient wife.

Her biggest problem now was what to wear. There were so many clothes in her dressing room. The rails were packed and the drawers were full. There was every accessory money could buy, and swimwear better suited to a supermodel. She chose one of the plainer costumes, and a sundress to wear over it. She was exploring the inside of a drawer when she came across a beautiful enamelled casket, decorated in shades of turquoise, jade green and violet, and gasped when she opened it to find a treasure trove of jewels. Rubies glistened against her skin like drops of blood, while sapphires sparkled as she held them up to the light. Emeralds flared and opals flashed fire, but for some reason they made her feel lonelier than ever. She didn't need all this extravagance, and would have traded every jewel in the world to have breakfast with her husband on this, the first morning of their married life.

Silence surrounded her as she ran the chains and

bracelets through her fingers. The jewels were fabulous, but they couldn't satisfy the practical woman she had become. Like the clothes and all the facilities on board, she felt, they were just toys to keep her happy. She looked at her simple wedding ring again, and turned it around her finger, knowing she would always love that best of all.

But she wasn't going to sit around feeling sorry for herself while Xavier was away. A sun hat and bare feet later, and she was ready to explore the ship.

He wasn't flying to the mainland on business as Rosie probably thought. Xavier was flying to the coast, and from there, out to the island. She was right in saying he didn't need to work on any particular day. His worldwide business was a well-oiled machine that allowed him to take time off whenever it suited him. What suited him now was space from Rosie. She'd really thrown him with the way she'd made him feel. He had shocked himself by wondering, when she'd stood beside him at the altar, if he loved her. It sure as hell wasn't indigestion digging away at his heart, then or now.

He landed the helicopter on the beach and then went for a walk, and after that a swim. He'd forgotten how good it felt to be on the island, free from the concerns of the outside world. It was therapeutic just sitting on the rocks, gazing out to sea. He rarely slowed down his pace of life these days, but the island demanded that he must.

He was beginning to see Isla Del Rey as Rosie must have seen it on her first day here, though he guessed that after the orphanage her experience must have been magnified tenfold. The island was startlingly beautiful; something else he'd forgotten over the years. There were deep ravines and rushing rivers, placid lakes and thick forest. Yes, the old house and grounds were badly run-down, but it was definitely worth saving. Old friends from the island, whom he hadn't seen for years, had opened his eyes at the wedding, clapping him on the back and complimenting him on his choice of bride. They told him that they had faith in Señorita Clifton, or Doña Rosa, as they had taken to calling Rosie on the island.

He stood and turned his face to the sun. The island's lush bounty was boundless. It was the perfect place to bring up a child. He had closed his mind to that possibility because of his own experience with parents who didn't want him. He accepted now that that had left a bitter mark, but not an indelible mark, thanks to Rosie. He could see the island afresh because of her. Even the ocean was a contradiction that reminded him of her. The water was a clear, tranquil blue today, but it could so quickly turn to furious grey—

He spun around as one of the elders of the island called to him.

'*Va a comer con nosotros, Xavier?*'

Would he care to eat with the family? He certainly

would. It would be a great honour, he called back, pleased to think they still cared about him.

He hadn't wanted to come back to Isla Del Rey, but he had. He hadn't wanted to care for the island, but he did. He hadn't wanted to care for anyone, because his experience of love had been so negative, but he cared for Rosie. He smiled as he thought about her as he fell into step with his elderly host. He didn't just care for Rosie Clifton—what was the point in denying it any longer? He loved her.

Time passed quickly on the balcony of his old friend's family home. Several generations had insisted on joining them, and they had laid out a feast to thank Xavier for inviting them to his wedding. He could hardly refuse their hospitality, and stayed until the screeching seagulls overhead in search of their supper reminded him that Rosie was still waiting for him on the ship.

She'd dressed for dinner. She'd never dressed for dinner in her life. She'd had no call to, but on one of her many exploratory missions around the ship she had spotted the stewards laying out a dining table beneath the stars. They were unfolding the finest white linen and adding a last polish to gleaming silver cutlery. Candles glowed in tall silver sconces, while beautiful flower arrangements had materialised seemingly out of nowhere, so she could hardly rock up in her jeans. The dress she had chosen from the vast selection in her dressing room was really beautiful. Made of soft ivory chiffon, it finished around knee length and had a nipped-in waist with quite a low neck. But the style was lovely, rather than obvious, and she had left her hair loose, as Xavier preferred it. She was still barefoot. He liked that too. She'd had a good day at sea, but had missed him, and however many times she told herself that she understood why he'd had to go, she really didn't, though something told her they would both have to compromise in this most unusual marriage.

She sat down to dinner. The stewards acknowledged her with polite smiles.

One asked what she would like to drink, and then stood back in the shadows as another poured her a glass of water. She couldn't think what else to say. She didn't want to start eating in case Xavier arrived, so she had to ignore her stomach's growls of complaint.

As time wore on and the sky grew inky black, she began to feel embarrassed. The stewards were still standing motionless, waiting for their next instruction. She was a new bride, barely one day married. They must be wondering if Xavier had had enough of her already. He probably had, Rosie thought, her stomach clenching with concern. She was young, broke, and unsophisticated. She brought nothing but her passion to the marriage. Though Xavier hadn't seemed disappointed last night, she reassured herself. He'd been so caring and sexy.

She tapped her fingers on the table as more doubts

set in. The candles were slowly burning down as she strained her ears for signs of the helicopter returning, and she almost jumped out of her skin when she heard the buzz of rotor blades approaching. Now she was angry with herself for being so self-obsessed. What if Xavier had had a problem, and that was why he was late?

The stewards rushed to move her chair as she bolted from the table.

'I'll be back,' she called out happily. One good thing that had resulted from her in-depth study of the vessel was that she could find her way to the helipad blindfolded.

He landed and saw Rosie at once. He wanted her with a madness that consumed him. He wanted to tell her about the things he'd been planning on his way back. 'You waited for me,' he said, embracing her.

'Xavier, I—'

Taking hold of her arm, he led her straight across the deck and down to their stateroom.

'Xavier—'

He slammed the door behind them. Pressing her back with the weight of his body, he silenced her with a hungry kiss.

'Xavier, you can't—'

'What can't I do?' he demanded, brushing the wisp of a dress from her shoulders. There was no need to rip it, as it fell off at a touch. Her skin felt so smooth and warm beneath his hands. The memory of her body was still so fresh in his mind. She was so beautiful and desirable, and he was so painfully erect.

'Xavier!'

Something in her tone stopped him dead.

'What's wrong with you?' she demanded in a tight, angry voice. 'You left me alone all day, and now this? You have to work. I get it. I understand that your work might take longer than you thought, but couldn't you have let me know you were safe? I was worried about you.' She searched his face with frustration. 'You could have contacted the ship,' she insisted. 'I'm not angry for myself, but your stewards have been hanging around all night, waiting for you.' When he didn't answer she got angry. 'Don't you care for anyone but yourself? This is the first full day of our honeymoon—'

On top of his frustration, tension, and his monumental decision to turn both his plans and his life upside down, Rosie's accusations were the straw that broke the camel's back. 'Ours is an arrangement— *an arrangement*!' he roared. 'I don't have to explain my every move to you.'

And now she had tears in her eyes, and he wasn't proud of that. 'I'm sorry.' He had never asked another human being to forgive him in his life. There had never been any call for him to do so, and now he'd upset the one person he should protect to his last breath.

Rosie was in no mood to forgive him. She was firing on all cylinders, chin raised, eyes blazing, 'An arrangement to suit you,' she accused him, 'because a man as unfeeling as you could never get an heir any other way.'

She hated saying words like that. The expression in Xavier's eyes wounded her as much as she'd wounded him, but she had to get through to him somehow. Leaving her so soon after their passionate wedding night, with no proper explanation, had cut her to the bone. 'Was that just part of our bargain when you made love to me last night?' she asked him. 'You did make love to me. Please tell me I'm not mistaken about that.' She hated the note of desperation in her voice. 'So, what am I to think?' she demanded when Xavier said nothing. 'You love having sex with me, and you love having me around for the challenge and the banter, but you'll never be able to love me in the way I need to be loved.'

'What way is that, Rosie?' he asked quietly.

She sucked in a breath as she searched her mind for the right words to express her feelings. 'I want to be loved fiercely, wildly, passionately—I don't even know,' she admitted, raking her hair with frustration.

'Do you think I'm so different from you?' Xavier demanded. 'Do I have different needs? Are you asking me to believe you entered into our agreement for anything less than one hundred per cent of the island? Or was it my finer qualities that tipped the balance for you? Perhaps the truth is, you would stop at nothing to get your share increased—and enjoy my lifestyle while you're at it?'

'That's not fair,' she exclaimed.

'So I'm not entitled to have the same doubts as you? You dream because it's safe—

'That's right, leave!' he stormed as she turned for the door.

Like his mother before her, Rosie thought, halting abruptly. 'I'm not going anywhere,' she said. 'I don't run away from anything. I never have. You have to bloom where you're planted, I was told at the orphanage, and that's what I'm going to do here.'

Her heart ached for both of them. Xavier was right in saying that neither of them was prepared to risk expressing their feelings, but there was one thing she had to get straight. 'I've never been interested in your money, or your lifestyle. From what I've seen, you've got everything and nothing. It doesn't matter if you drink out of crystal glasses on your super-yacht, or a plastic beaker at the orphanage. Life is empty, if you shun love and go through it alone.'

'You're an expert on feelings now?' he said, with a lift of his brow.

'I only know what I feel in here.' She touched her chest. 'And you can say what you like about Doña Anna, but I think she threw us together in one last attempt to jolt both of us onto a better track.'

'My aunt didn't have a romantic bone in her body.'

'That shows how little you knew her.'

'Are you saying you knew her better than me?' Xavier demanded with disbelief.

'I did,' she said bluntly. 'Did you never wonder why Doña Anna lived alone?'

'I was her nephew, not her agony aunt. Of course I didn't know.'

'Did it never occur to you that your aunt had a lot of love to give, or did you just see her as a grouchy old lady who brought you up because there was no one else who was prepared to step up and do that?'

'Maybe,' Xavier admitted, frowning. 'But how does that change anything?'

'Did you know that her fiancé was killed just before they were due to be married, or that he was the love of her life?'

'I didn't know.' And he was shocked to learn that his aunt had been left alone and lonely, until Rosie had arrived on the island.

'We grew close when I read to your aunt in the library—that was when she told me that books were her escape. She went on to explain why she felt the need to escape.'

'*Dios,*' Xavier murmured beneath his breath. 'I had no idea.'

'And no reason why you should. I doubt Doña Anna would have confided in her nephew, even if you had never left her side.'

'So, what are you saying?'

'She could only put the pieces into play. She couldn't direct us from the grave.'

'Couldn't she?' He huffed a humourless laugh. 'This seems typical of her mischief to me.'

'Was she ever malicious, as far as you know?'

'Never,' he admitted. 'Not in all the time I knew her.'

'Then why would she do this if she hadn't wanted us to be together?'

And now she'd said too much. Or maybe not...

Rosie's heart lifted as Xavier pulled away from the wall, but then it clenched with despair as he turned without another word and left the room.

CHAPTER SIXTEEN

HE STOOD ON the deck, staring out to sea, wondering where they'd be now if their life experiences had been different. His best guess was that his aunt and Rosie would have found each other somehow, and that Rosie would be on the island right now, doing everything she could to help the islanders even with zero funds and only her eternal optimism driving her forward.

He certainly wouldn't have come up with the plan that he had. If his childhood had been different, he would have visited the island regularly and felt comfortable there, instead of harking back to the bitter memories of childhood disappointment. Rosie had made him confront things he hadn't thought about for years, which was ironic when her childhood made his seem idyllic by comparison, and the wounds he lived with nothing more than an indulgence.

He had to put the past to good purpose now, as she had, and use those lessons to move forward. She was right in saying that wealth meant nothing unless it could do some good, and life was certainly diminished without someone to share it with.

He hadn't intended to make her unhappy. He hadn't even realised how unhappy she was, but now he felt her pain as keenly as his own. All that mattered to him, he had discovered, was Rosie's happiness. His ring was on her finger, and Rosie was in his bed, but what would it take to win her heart?

Doubt was still hammering down on her the next morning. She'd slept alone. Xavier hadn't been near their stateroom, which left her with the growing suspicion that she had damaged something precious, like a green shoot she'd carelessly trodden down beneath the heel of her shoe. As she stood beneath the shower, she felt the loss of him keenly. She wanted the comfort of his arms, the thrill of his body, and the caring individual she'd increasingly seen emerge in him. The one thing she had never once considered was giving up—not on her relationship with Xavier, and not on her commitment to the island. So it was time to swallow her pride, get dressed, and go to find him.

Don Xavier was in his study, one of the stewards told her.

'Rosie.' Xavier stood as she opened the door. 'Please. Come in…'

She felt his warmth reaching out to her. He was standing behind the desk at the far end of the room.

Even in shadow, he was the most compelling man she'd *ever* met, Rosie concluded wistfully.

'Is something wrong?' he asked.

'Just that I wish I knew you better,' she admitted. 'I wish I knew what made you tick.'

'That's easy,' he said.

'Is it?' She stood by the door, knowing that if she came any closer her feelings would overwhelm her.

'We're the same, you and I,' he said.

She shook her head ruefully. 'I don't think so. You're frightened of feeling.'

'Whereas you have no difficulty in expressing yourself,' he countered with a wry look.

She knew one thing for certain. She would rather spend the rest of her life getting over Xavier than another night on the ship without him. She wanted to be close to him, to be one with him in every way there was.

'You came here to say something?' he prompted.

Yes, and the air was so still, it seemed as if the whole world were listening in. She didn't know where to begin. Xavier was impossible to know, and impossible to live without.

'Rosie?' he prompted.

'I want to understand you,' she said.

'Then take a look in the mirror,' he suggested.

She frowned. 'We couldn't be more different, you and I. Parental love and family solidarity might seem like Shangri-La to me, but I'm not ready to give up on my dreams yet.'

'What do you mean?' His voice was soft, his stare intent. 'Are you saying I'm not capable of loving a child?'

'Are you?'

Coming around the desk, he stood in front of her. 'We should give it a chance—give us a chance. You're as bad as me. You shut out feelings too, and if they creep up on you you tell yourself it's another of your fantasies, and that makes them easier to deal with.'

'Maybe,' she accepted. 'But how can we give this a chance? How can it work between us? You and your six-star hotels, and your lavish marinas, and me with my vegetable plots?'

Xavier's face warmed. 'You don't know my plans.'

'Then why don't you tell me? We should work together.'

'Do you think that's what my aunt intended all along?'

Hope was a fragile thing, and she wasn't ready to commit fully yet. 'Maybe Doña Anna expected more of me than I can give.'

'No.' Xavier shook his head decisively. 'I don't believe that for a moment. Everyone has doubts. It's what drives us forward. You're stronger than you know, Rosie.'

'So you believe in me?'

'Isn't that obvious?' Cupping her chin, Xavier made her look at him. His eyes were warm and full of everything she needed to see. 'You're the strongest woman I've ever met. Don't let the past bring you down, Rosie. Isn't that what you'd like to tell me? I know you love the island—everyone knows it—but what about something for you? You don't have to give all the time. Sometimes people want to do things for you, and sometimes you have to let them.'

'Forgive me,' she whispered, closing her eyes. 'I know you had a lousy childhood, just as I know what we both owe Doña Anna.'

'Do you trust me, Rosie? On our wedding night you said you did.'

'I did. I do,' she said, staring that trust into Xavier's eyes.

'Tell me what you want—what you really want.'

I want you, she thought. *I want you to love me. I want you to put your arms around me. I want to believe you, if you tell me that you want me to stay. I want to have a child we both love and care for, not a child that's been manufactured just to continue a family line.*

'Say it, Rosie. Don't just think it. Say it out loud.'

He was asking her to risk her heart, and the words she so desperately wanted to say stalled on her lips. She just couldn't get them out. And then she had a light-bulb moment, and she realised what Xavier was trying to get her to do. They were both locked up on their individual islands, and it was up to each of them to break free.

She began haltingly. Tiny steps towards sharing her feelings, something she'd never done before. 'I want this to be real between us,' she admitted. 'I want to say what I think, instead of hiding my feelings from you all the time—' It was almost a relief, she discovered, this letting go, and as she gained in confidence her words gathered pace. 'I want to tell you how you make me feel, and not have you laugh at me—'

'Laugh at you?' Xavier interrupted, frowning.

'Yes,' Rosie admitted. She was quiet for quite some time, and then she added softly, 'I want to tell you that I love you.'

'Say that again,' Xavier insisted.

'I want to tell you that I love you,' she repeated in a louder, clearer voice.

'And?' he prompted.

'And why am I the only one doing this?' she protested, only half teasing him.

'My turn will come?' he suggested with a smile.

'I want to tell you that I know what you're trying to do, and that I agree that until each of us can free ourselves from the past, neither of us is going anywhere, as individuals, or as a couple, however temporary our marriage might be, or even as joint owners of Isla Del Rey. The past will always hold us back, hold us down—we both have to change, and maybe we've got a long way to go before we can do that. I want us both to speak openly, for good and for bad, and without editing every comment first. I want to share everything with you, but I can't, because I get frightened—'

'You? Frightened?' Xavier's look was disbelieving.

'Frightened you'll think I'm stupid,' Rosie admitted.

'Never.' Slanting his sexy smile, Xavier shook his head. 'You're like a light shining so bright you almost blinded me. And it was definitely a light I didn't want to see. You blinded me with your honesty, and left me questioning what I've been doing with my life. 'So, why don't you ask me about my plans for the island?'

She hardly dared to ask. 'What have you done?'

'We're sailing there now,' he said, 'so you'll see for yourself. The islanders are planning a fiesta in our honour to celebrate our marriage. They want us to have a proper celebration, amongst friends.'

'Tell me about your plans first,' Rosie insisted.

'Okay. I'm going to create a kids' centre on the island in honour of my aunt. She always wanted me to do something useful with my money. At the time I was too busy amassing a fortune to work out what she meant. I was so desperate not to end up like my parents—always with their hands in someone else's pocket—so money meant everything to me then. But this is going to be a non-profit-making scheme. It will be the perfect tribute to a woman I neglected in life, and am determined to honour in death. How do you feel about going in with me on that?'

'Are you serious?' Rosie was stunned. 'I'd love to. What changed your mind?'

'You did,' Xavier admitted. 'When I went back to the island yesterday, I saw everything through your eyes, and then I understood what the island really needed, and what I could bring to it.'

Reaching out, he drew her close. Her face and her body tingled. Staring into her eyes, he dipped his head and kissed her long and slow. When he pulled back, he said, 'I love you, Rosie. I'd do anything to make you happy. I've loved you from the moment I first saw you on that beach—I just didn't know what those feelings were.'

'You only knew I annoyed the hell out of you?' she suggested, starting to smile.

Xavier laughed. A bolt of sheer happiness lit up his face. 'No one had ever held me at bay before,' he admitted. 'I hadn't felt that angry for years. I hadn't felt anything for years. I was furious at being dragged back to an island that made me remember my childhood and my parents, and all my mixed-up feelings. And then there was the indignity of having to share the island with my aunt's housekeeper. How ridiculous,' he said, embracing her warmly. 'How arrogant I was. My only thought was to drive you away as fast as I could.'

'And now?' she whispered.

'And now I have to keep you by any means possible. What would it take to do that, Rosie? What would it take to make ours a real marriage?'

She looked at him. 'Just love me.'

* * *

As they arrived at Isla Del Rey a crowd was waiting for them on the dock. It was entirely different from the formal gathering of dignitaries who had attended their wedding in the cathedral. These were people Rosie knew and loved. Everyone had dressed up for the occasion. It was party night on Isla Del Rey. There was nothing the islanders loved more than a celebration, and they must have pooled their limited resources to give them a welcome like this. She was touched by the effort they'd gone to, and so very happy to be back on the island she loved. This was special, she thought as she walked down the gang-plank hand in hand with Xavier.

An even bigger surprise awaited her as Xavier had organised a blessing of their vows. Taking hold of both her hands in his, he searched her eyes. A yearning grew inside him as they stared at each other, and he knew in that moment that his life and everything in it depended on the answer Rosie would give him.

'Are you happy to renew your vows?' Xavier asked.

'Oh, yes,' she said, smiling deep into his eyes.

A happy grin spread across his face.

'Are *you* sure about this?' she asked him discreetly. 'Are you sure you want me to renew our vows with me barefoot in a sundress with a rose in my hair?'

'I've never seen you looking more beautiful, or more Rosie-like.' He squeezed her hand to reassure her as a notary halted in front of them.

'Do you have the ring you spoke of?' the notary asked him.

'I have it,' Xavier confirmed, pulling the piece of string out of his pocket. 'Will this do?'

'Very nicely,' the man agreed with a warm smile for Rosie.

The simple renewal of their wedding vows meant so much to Rosie, it was her dream come true: standing next to the man she loved, the man who had just told her how much he loved her, in front of people who genuinely cared for both of them. If she had ever needed proof that her optimistic take on life was justified, this was it. She only had to look around to see that their happiness was infectious. Even with all the money in the world to spend on a celebration, nothing could be better than this. It was the happiest night of her life.

The party afterwards was the best fun ever. And as they came together for the last dance of the night the islanders formed a circle around them. They weren't looking for sensation or gossip, they just wanted to join in and wish them well. No one on Isla Del Rey was ever afraid to show their feelings and Rosie would never be frightened to do so again.

They spent the night at the hacienda with the windows open so they could hear the night sounds: owls hooting, cicadas chirruping, as they made love in time to the surf.

'I've got another surprise for you,' Xavier murmured.

'What is it?' she demanded, a smile spreading across her face.

'A proper Christmas, just for you and me—a second honeymoon with no distractions.'

'Christmas?' Rosie's eyes fired with wonder as the child inside her got its dream come true at last.

'Big and brazen,' he insisted, 'with too many gifts, and a turkey that's far too big for us. Mince pies, and Yule logs. Crackers and tinsel. Would you like that?'

'I'd love that,' she said and her eyes filled with tears. 'I love you.'

Much, much later, they talked about the children's centre Xavier had planned, and he told her the hacienda would be the perfect headquarters. He explained what he'd like her to do at the children's centre. 'So, I'm to be an assistant to the superintendent of the facility? That sounds very grand.' Rosie frowned. 'Can I still be barefoot, or do I have to wear a suit?'

'You can wear whatever you like.'

'There's just one thing.'

'Yes?'

She braced herself to tell him. 'I might need maternity leave.'

'Might?' Xavier shot her a wry look. 'I'm counting on it.'

'That's not what I…'

'Are you telling me you're pregnant?' He held her at arm's length to stare into her eyes, as if they would tell him the truth. 'How can you be sure? So soon?' he demanded, taut with hope.

Forget his half of the island—forget everything! His head was reeling at the possibility that Rosie was pregnant. Everything exploded into vivid colour. His fears of parenting evaporated. If he was useless, he could learn. He had Doña Anna's example to draw on and Rosie at his side. No one got a manual with their first child, so he was level pegging with everyone else, learning as he went along.

'It's too soon to be sure,' Rosie warned him, seeing the joy on his face. 'I've just got this feeling...'

'I think we'd better get you checked out.'

'Are you pleased?'

Was he pleased? Whatever he had expected to feel when they had first entered into this so-called arrangement was nothing approaching this. He was speechless and drowning in emotion.

'Xavier? Say something—are you all right?'

'I am beyond all right—beyond happy—beyond anything I've ever felt before. Please, let this be true.' He grasped hold of Rosie's hands when no words seem adequate. 'Do you need to sit down?'

'I'm lying down, in case you hadn't noticed.' They laughed with sheer happiness, and hugged each other. 'And I'm pregnant, not sick,' she said when he eventually let her go. 'If I'm right, you'll get the heir you need.'

'Don't!' he exclaimed, frowning. 'Please don't say that. Don't remind me of what an idiot I've been— it's bad for my ego.' She laughed and kissed him again. 'I've got you, Rosie, and that's all I care about. I've got the woman I want, and the only mother I could ever want for my children. You've made me the happiest man in the world. You'll have the best care available.'

'You don't need to tell me that,' Rosie assured him, catching hold of his hand. 'I've got you.'

EPILOGUE

ROSIE RECEIVED CONFIRMATION from the island's doctor that she was pregnant a short time before Christmas. The doctor also confirmed Rosie's suspicion that sometimes a woman just knew these things. There was no medical reason that could account for that feeling of hers. It was in the bones, he said.

Her baby would be born in the late spring, and, with the whole world at his disposal, Xavier had declared that if they were going to celebrate Christmas properly there must be snow, and so he piloted the jet to the land of cuckoo clocks and chocolate. Even the flight over the snow-clad mountains was spectacular, but Xavier's chalet, with its long winding drive, lined by Christmas trees, each one lit with tiny shimmering lights, was magical. The burnished wood construction, with its steeply sloping roof and quaint painted shutters at every window, was the perfect setting for the perfect Christmas, Rosie thought as they drew up outside. Lanterns glowed on either side of the front door, and a Christmas wreath of pine cones and cinnamon sticks, secured with blousy bows of vivid red ribbon, welcomed them as Xavier helped her out of the rugged four-wheeler.

'What's this?' she asked as he pressed a small box into her hands.

'Your first Christmas present.'

She laughed. 'My first?'

'Get used to it, Señora Del Rio. There are twelve days of Christmas, but you'll have to forgive me in this instance for getting ahead of the game, but I had no alternative if we're to get inside the chalet. Don't worry,' he added, 'some of the gifts might be in kind. I don't want to overburden you with luggage,' he explained with a wicked grin.

'So long as it's not that wretched ring,' she warned, shooting a wary glance at the box.

'Why don't you open it and find out?' Xavier suggested.

She did just that, and pulled out a key.

'Welcome home, Señora Del Rio.'

'I don't understand.'

'This is your house. Any time you want to get away from me you can come here—'

'You're giving me a house?' Rosie exclaimed. She couldn't take it in.

'A Swiss chalet,' he said. 'Just the first of many gifts for my beautiful wife.'

He silenced her protests with a kiss, and made her sigh with pleasure as he caressed her cheek. 'You don't play fair,' she complained softly as he nuzzled the very sensitive skin just below her ear, making her shiver with arousal.

'And I don't take no for an answer, either,' he reminded her.

'But you can't give me a house. It's too much.'

'I can and I have,' he argued firmly. 'This is going to be the best Christmas either of us has ever had.'

'It will be. I promise,' Rosie confirmed, determined to do everything she could to make it so.

'Why don't you open your front door, *señora*?'

'I suppose if this is my house I'd better show you around—'

'Why don't we start with the bedrooms?'

'Do you seriously think we'll get that far…?'

The front door opened on a magical scene. A roaring log fire welcomed them inside the beautiful house, and Xavier carried her over the threshold. Floor-to-ceiling windows overlooked the snow-covered mountains, while the décor in rich, warm shades promised that this would be the cosiest of homes in which to spend the holiday season.

'What's in all these boxes?' Rosie asked as she took stock of them.

'A ready-decorated home would be too easy for you, my beautiful, romantic wife,' Xavier told her as he lowered her down and stripped off her warm coat. 'And so I've provided all the ingredients you could possibly need to dream up whatever scheme you want.'

'Christmas decorations,' she exclaimed. 'Can we decorate the chalet together?'

'I wouldn't have it any other way,' Xavier said as he tossed his heavy outer jacket on a chair. 'Shall we make a start?'

'I meant you should help me with the Christmas decorations,' she chastised him as he brought her into his arms.

'We've got all night for that,' he reminded her, brushing her lips with his.

Rosie couldn't have been happier with their cosy nest. They were in their own little world, far away from the glare of public scrutiny. 'You couldn't have chosen anywhere better. I love it. We can be Mr and Mrs Normal here.'

'Correction—I can be Mr Normal,' he argued. He smiled against her mouth as he whispered, 'There's no hope for you…'

Grabbing hold of his arms, she attempted to give him a little shake, but he was rock. Her need soared. 'That rug looks so neglected…'

They cooked Christmas dinner together with the help of a stack of advice from celebrity chefs who had rushed to offer Xavier their congratulations, no doubt in hope of securing franchises at one of his many hotels. They had to be very strict with themselves to make sure the celebratory meal didn't burn in what had quickly turned into a highly charged second honeymoon. When it came to it, they ended up naked, eating off the same plate on the rug in front of the roaring fire.

Rosie was concerned that her Christmas gift for Xavier wasn't enough. He had assured her on numerous occasions that their baby was more than enough for every Christmas going forward. Their child was a blessing, as well as the most wonderful gift, but in practical terms Rosie wanted him to have something to open on Christmas Day. And how could she ever compete with the chocolate-box-perfect Swiss Chalet he had given her? She could only hope that her modest gifts would please him.

'I've got another small gift for you,' Xavier admitted as Rosie brought out a neatly wrapped package.

'See you, and raise you one,' she said, smiling as she lifted out a bulkier package from under the bed.

'This is the perfect Christmas Day,' Xavier said as he ripped the paper off her first gift. 'Rosie…' He stared down with astonishment at the books she'd given him.

'Do you like them?'

'First editions of my favourite author—are you serious? I love them.'

'Margaret helped me—told me which antiquarian bookshop to use. They're for the library on the island,' she explained. 'You don't have these volumes, do you?'

'Do you know how rare these are?'

She had some idea. It was only when Margaret had insisted that Rosie must enjoy some of the money from her inheritance that she had been able to afford them.

'What's this?' she asked as Xavier handed her a package that looked very much like the one she was about to give to him.

'Open it and see,' he said.

He opened his second gift at the same time, only to discover they'd both had the same idea. Rosie's bright red Christmas sweater had a cross-eyed reindeer on the front, while the one she had given Xavier had a smiling Father Christmas with rosy cheeks and a long grey beard.

'Perfect!' they chorused, laughing as they fell back on the pillows.

'But I don't think we need to put them on just yet, do you?' Xavier murmured, reaching for her.

Five years later...

The sugar-sand beach on sunny Isla Del Rey was packed with islanders, visitors, children, and young people of all ages. The hacienda had been completely renovated, remaining true to its original architectural features, and there was a sturdy handrail on the impeccably maintained cliff path.

Xavier held a barbecue on the beach once a year to host all the suppliers and buyers, who were big supporters of the island's now famous organic vegetable farm. He cooked and the older children from the thriving Doña Anna Adventure Camp helped him out.

This year's beach-feast was the biggest celebration yet, as it marked the opening of the third building for their international centre. Interested parties had arrived on the island from all over the world to pick up tips on the magic that turned troubled youngsters into confident young people.

Xavier would have said that it was the Rosie touch. Her eternal optimism meant that she had never given up on a child yet. In Rosie's opinion, the success of the centre was all Xavier's doing. He had the drive, the vision, and the practical skills, while she was the dreamer who provided the barefoot fun. Of course, one of their secret weapons was Xavier's trusted financial director, Margaret, who, having semi-retired from full-time work, was helping them to run the centre.

'You're not a bad chef,' Rosie commented with a grin as Elijah, the four-year-old at her feet, clamoured for another treat from Daddy's kitchen. Their two-year-old twins, Lily and Grace, were just happy to take everything in, while the bump in her stomach was too busy having a kick-boxing fest all its own to be in a position to ask for something to munch on.

'Happy?' Xavier asked, wiping his muscular forearm across his brow. He could only grant himself the briefest of breaks, but the break had to be long enough to kiss his wife. That was his rule.

'What do you think?' Rosie teased.

'I think I love you, Señora Del Rio,' Xavier whispered, staring deep into Rosie's amethyst eyes.

'That's a relief,' she teased softly. Holding Xavier's dark, sexy stare, she hitched Elijah up onto one hip. 'Because I adore you, *señor*, and I always will.'

* * * * *

If you enjoyed this story, check out these other
great reads from Susan Stephens:
IN THE SHEIKH'S SERVICE
BOUND TO THE TUSCAN BILLIONAIRE
BACK IN THE BRAZILIAN'S BED

And don't miss these other
WEDLOCKED! themed stories:
TRAPPED BY VIALLI'S VOWS
by Chantelle Shaw
WEDDED, BEDDED, BETRAYED
by Michelle Smart
Available now!

#3485 THE PRINCE'S PREGNANT MISTRESS
Heirs Before Vows
by Maisey Yates

"I'm pregnant." It takes two words to see Prince Raphael DeSantis bound to a *waitress*. Now to prevent an international incident, Raphael must marry his mistress! But heartsore Bailey won't come willingly. Raphael must seduce Bailey Harper into submission...

#3486 THE GUARDIAN'S VIRGIN WARD
One Night With Consequences
by Caitlin Crews

Domineering Spaniard Izar Agustin couldn't have imagined that his ward, innocent Liliana Girard Brooks, would become such an alluring woman. One night of sensual abandon shows Liliana the unconscious desires of her body... But the consequences of that night bind them together...forever!

#3487 THE DESERT KING'S SECRET HEIR
Secret Heirs of Billionaires
by Annie West

Surrounded by society's glitterati, Arden Wills is confronted with her first and only love, Idris Baddour—a man she never knew was a sheikh! When their ardent kiss is blasted across the world's media, Arden's secret comes to light—the Sheikh has a son!

#3488 SURRENDERING TO THE VENGEFUL ITALIAN
Irresistible Mediterranean Tycoons
by Angela Bissell

Not even his foe's stunning daughter, Helena Shaw, will halt Leonardo Vincenti's vengeance. Leo knows that Helena would never willingly return to his side, so he blackmails her. But the passion that undid them before soon forces them *both* to the brink of surrender...

YOU CAN FIND MORE INFORMATION ON UPCOMING HARLEQUIN® TITLES, FREE EXCERPTS AND MORE AT WWW.HARLEQUIN.COM.

HPCNM1116RB

*Natalia Di Sione hasn't left the family estate in years,
but she must retrieve her grandfather's lost book of
poems from Angelos Menas! The lives of the brooding
Greek and his daughter were changed irrevocably by
a fire, and Talia finds herself drawn to the formidable
tycoon. She knows the untold pleasure Angelos offers
is limited, but when she leaves with the book, will her
heart remain on the island?*

Read on for a sneak preview of
A DI SIONE FOR THE GREEK'S PLEASURE,
*the sixth in the unmissable new eight book
Harlequin Presents® series*
THE BILLIONAIRE'S LEGACY.

"Talia…" Angelos's voice broke on her name, and then,
before she could even process what was happening, he
pulled her toward him, his hands hard on her shoulders as his
mouth crashed down on hers and plundered its soft depths.

It had been ten years since she'd been kissed, and then
only a schoolboy's buss. She'd never been kissed like this,
never felt every sense blaze to life, every nerve ending tingle
with awareness, nearly painful in its intensity, as Angelos's
mouth moved on hers and he pulled her tightly to him.

His hard contours collided against her softness, each
point of contact creating an unbearably exquisite ache of
longing as she tangled her hands in his hair and fit her mouth
against his.

She was a clumsy, inexpert kisser, not sure what to do
with her lips or tongue, only knowing that she wanted more
of this. Of him.

She felt his hand slide down to cup her breast, his palm hot and hard through the thin material of her dress, and a gasp of surprise and delight escaped her.

That small sound of pleasure was enough to jolt Angelos out of his passion-fogged daze, for he dropped his hand and in one awful, abrupt movement tore his mouth from hers and stepped back.

"I'm sorry," he said, his voice coming out in a ragged gasp.

"No…" Talia pressed one shaky hand to her buzzing lips as she tried to blink the world back into focus. "Don't be sorry," she whispered. "It was wonderful."

"I shouldn't have—"

"Why not?" she challenged. She felt frantic with the desperate need to feel and taste him again, and more important, not to have him withdraw from her, not just physically, but emotionally. Angelos didn't answer and she forced herself to ask the question again. "Why not, Angelos?"

"Because you are my employee, and I was taking advantage of you," he gritted out. "It was not appropriate…"

"I don't care about appropriate," she cried. She knew she sounded desperate and even pathetic but she didn't care. She wanted him. She needed him. "I care about you," she confessed, her voice dropping to a choked whisper, and surprise and something worse flashed across Angelos's face. He shook his head, the movement almost violent and terribly final.

"No, Talia," he told her flatly. "You don't."

Don't miss
A DI SIONE FOR THE GREEK'S PLEASURE,
available December 2016 wherever
Harlequin Presents® books and ebooks are sold.

www.Harlequin.com

HARLEQUIN

Presents®

*Christmas might be a time for giving,
but in Lynne Graham's festive new duet*
Christmas with a Tycoon, *two Mediterranean
billionaires are thinking only of what they can take!*

Italian tycoon Vito Zaffari is waiting out the festive season
while a family scandal fades from the press. So he's come to his
friend's snow-covered English country cottage, determined to
shut out the world.

Until a beautiful bombshell dressed as Santa literally crashes into his
Christmas! Innocent Holly Cleaver sneaks under Vito's defenses—he
wants her like no other woman before and decides he *must* have her.

When Vito finds her gone the next day he's sure she'll be easy to
forget…until he discovers that their one night of passion has a
shocking Christmas consequence!

Don't miss

THE GREEK'S
CHRISTMAS BRIDE

December 2016!

Stay Connected:
www.Harlequin.com
www.IHeartPresents.com

 /HarlequinBooks
 @HarlequinBooks
 /HarlequinBooks

HP13488